THE·SPHINX
GOLDEN JUBILEE BOOK
OF MAGIC

A Selection of Tricks from the
Pages of the Magazine

Compiled by

MILBOURNE CHRISTOPHER

Illustrated by

SID LORRAINE

Published by

FLOSSO HORNMANN MAGIC CO.

Published by

FLOSSO HORNMANN MAGIC CO.

Printed in the

United States of America

Preface

When, one warm day this past summer, John Mulholland suggested the editing of this book I agreed with little hesitancy, thinking it would be a pleasant task to re-read the early volumes of "The Sphinx," a simple matter to prepare the best tricks for publication. Two weeks or so, I thought, would see the work through.

So I started through the 49 years. I had planned to read only the tricks, but the articles and pictures and news notes kept distracting me. Reports on the shows of Kellar and Herrmann intrigued me; the rise of young performers such as Thurston and Houdini, not to mention Dante and Blackstone; and most of my contemporaries kept side-tracking my attention from the matter in hand. Then the tricks themselves! Multiply one issue by more than five hundred and you begin to appreciate the problem of combining the best feats into a single book. It would have been far easier to compile five volumes than one. So many choice bits of conjuring had to be put aside. It would astonish you to check in current dealers' catalogues the many tricks which first appeared in "The Sphinx." A large and excellent group of tricks had to be by-passed because they were already so firmly established as the standard feats of today's sorcerers. Another batch of bafflers had to be put aside because, though the trap doors and special stage mechanisms on which they depended are just as practical today as they were several decades ago, there are few modern wizards who could put them to use. The decline of the theatre and the rise of television, hotel and intimate entertainment has made a special yard-stick necessary to measure the value of a feat today. The estimated two weeks stretched into months, but the manuscript began to take shape.

This book is far more than a collection of tricks; it's a procession of the outstanding performers, inventors and writers of magic from 1900 down to today. No one man could possibly have explored so many avenues with so many unusual results. Here then are not only outstanding tricks, but the outstanding men who are responsible for them telling you how to do them. Here is magic for all tastes, all purposes.

Milbourne Christopher

Introduction

It was "The Sphinx" which told me what went on inside magic when, as a very young magician, I could see only the outside. It was "The Sphinx" which brought me advice, from the very top people of magic, on how to better my performances. It was "The Sphinx" which gave me many of the feats of magic my audiences most enjoy. Therefore, as a performer, and one greatly interested in all phases of magic, the magazine has meant a great deal to me. I am not unique in my feeling for, during the half century that "The Sphinx" has been published, magicians everywhere have looked on the magazine as their key to the secret door of the world of magic. Just a few weeks ago William R. Walsh, America's number 1 amateur magician, wrote to me:

"Well do I remember the thrill experienced when, as a young man, I found my first issue of 'The Sphinx'—how I accumulated at first single copies, and then, later, volumes—the many, many evenings I pored over each article and advertisement—how it opened up an entirely new world for me, one of intrigue and deeply rooted interest. This all began about 1915. A few years before this I had been casually interested in magic, but this was the beginning of a real and consuming hobby which has been very close to my heart ever since. Now I am the possessor of a complete file of 'The Sphinx'."

In all the fifty years of publication of the magazine, there have been but three editors, and I feel that I was very fortunate to have known well both the first, Bill Hilliar, and Doc Wilson, the second. In 1912 I was pleased and honored when Doc asked me to work for his paper. I enjoyed working for Doc Wilson for eighteen years. It, also, has been a privilege and a pleasure to edit "The Sphinx" these past twenty-one years. The mechanical headaches of any given month are forgotten with the enthusiasm of working on the next issue.

When it was decided to publish a book to commemorate the 50th Anniversary Issue of "The Sphinx," to include some of the outstanding magical effects which first had appeared in the magazine, I was in a quandary. To quote the old proverb, "I could not see the forest for the trees." To me the vast majority of the tricks published in "The Sphinx" were well worth republishing. However, to publish so large a number was an utter impossibility. Therefore, I felt that the selection of a reasonable number should be left to one not so intimately connected with the magazine. Milbourne Christopher was given the huge task of making the selection. To make the book uniform and more attractive, Sid Lorraine drew a completely new set of illustrations.

Throughout the years, each editor, in turn, has been grateful for the help of the thousands of magicians who were willing to share their cherished and most excellent secrets.

I believe that you, and your audiences, will like the magic in this book, too.

John Mulholland

The Ne Plus Ultra Cabinet

By Harry Kellar

There are times when even the best posted, most practical magician has the extreme pleasure of witnessing during the performance of a brother wizard some illusion that simply dazzles him, so clever and (to him) so inexplicable it seems.

Such was my experience during one of my recent trips across the water. I was in one of Europe's largest cities. Several of the theatres had magicians on their programs and, as usual, when the opportunity offers itself, I started out to witness their exhibitions, hoping to see some new tricks and possibly get a pointer or two. My desire was fulfilled far beyond my wildest hopes or dreams. I went into a theatre where the magician was billed to perform "A series of most astounding spiritualistic phenomena, including the most marvelous materialization ever witnessed on a brilliantly lighted stage." Being especially interested in this class of work, I purchased a front seat and waited for the "Marvels."

After the usual thing of table tipping, slate writing, and ordinary tests, came the feature of his show. A cabinet (very similar to the one used by myself) about six feet square, say eight high, raised some eight or ten inches from the ground, was wheeled on the stage. This cabinet was composed of thin, light wood and made, you might say, entirely of doors. Each of the four sides was composed of two doors opening outwards. The cabinet was spun around to show all four sides. The professor then opened all the doors to show it entirely empty, then closing them after him, stepped from the cabinet and fired a pistol. The front doors flew open and a gentleman in full evening dress stepped out of the previously empty cabinet. Again all doors were opened and closed and again a man was suddenly produced, making two men from the empty frame. Once more all doors were opened; the performer bowed, leaving us to wonder from whence came the two gentlemen in the dress suits.

To me it was as puzzling an illusion as I ever saw. Explanations offered themselves to my mind in rapid succession and each seemed more impossible than the one before. After a couple of days, just as I was ready to give up in disgust, the true explanation came to me. After

I had my diagrams all drawn I went once more to see the trick done to verify my theory. I had struck it right.

As I said before, the cabinet is composed of a light, thin panelled wood, so made that the two doors on each side open outward. When the trick is begun the two men are wheeled on the stage inside of the closed cabinet. When set, the two back corners have a small ledge just large enough for a man to stand upon. Figure 1 shows a ground plan of the cabinet, all doors open; the men are indicated by the letters A and B. The dotted lines indicate the arcs described by the doors in opening. My explanation is given figuring from the rear of the cabinet, thus making the man B as right side, and A as left side. Now we are ready.

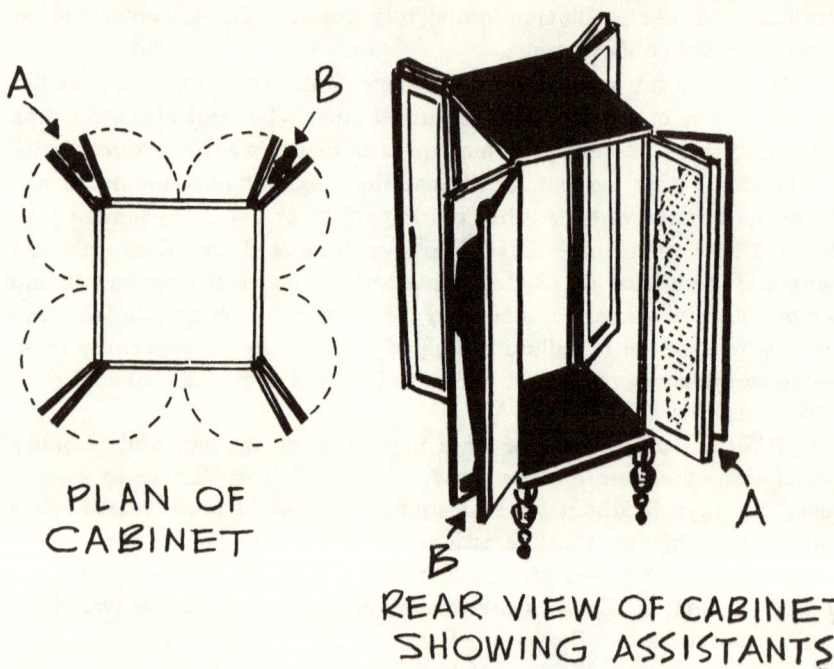

PLAN OF
CABINET

REAR VIEW OF CABINET
SHOWING ASSISTANTS
CONCEALED AT "A" "B"

Both men are in the cabinet, wheeled on stage and spun around. As the stage performer makes his announcement, the men step out on the back of the cabinet and the performer opens the front doors. He then opens the doors on the left side, which allows A to step into hiding. The left back door is now opened. A is concealed. The right side doors are opened, and B steps into position. The right back door is opened and B is concealed.

The performer closes the left side back door. A steps behind it. The left side doors are then closed, then the right side back door. B steps behind it, and the right side doors are closed. The performer steps out, closing the front doors behind him. As he does so, A opens the back door, steps inside, and at the shot of the pistol throws the front doors open and walks out.

The performer returns to the cabinet and opens the right side doors, on which B steps into position. The right side back door is now opened, then the left side and back doors. The right side back door is now opened, then the left side and back doors. The right side back door is closed, then the right side doors, then the left side and back doors. Again the performer closes the front doors as he steps to the stage.

B now duplicates the moves that A made. After his production, the doors are opened any way the performer sees fit, the cabinet is spun around and the illusion completed.

A Sleight and a Force

By David Devant

I always believe in simplifying the means of performing any illusion. Thus, I have always taught amateurs to eliminate the pass in card tricks. That is to say, as much as possible. For instance, it is usual to receive back a chosen card on the lower half of the pack. Then put the two halves together. Then make the pass, and then false shuffle the cards. I suggest the pass, in this instance, is not necessary. I receive back the card on the lower half, bring the top half to it, and keeping the two separated by the little finger of the left hand, leave it thus for a few seconds, then separate them again by commencing a false shuffle. To do this I naturally take the top half of the pack and drop it in front of the lower half. This leaves the chosen card on top and you continue to false shuffle by slipping the chosen card each time you transfer cards from the back to the front of the pack.

In the same way a simple method of forcing three cards is this, which I advise amateurs to use. Make up a pack consisting of groups of three cards, each group being similar cards. A pack like this may be cut as many times as you like and the same three cards will always be on top of either pack.

Take the pack down into the audience on a small tray and ask two or three persons to cut the cards and the last person who cuts to cut again. Thus leaving three packets of cards. Ask this last person to choose which packet shall be used, and get him to deal out three cards from the top of it, handing one each to the nearest persons. Then, gathering up the rest of the cards, you say you will turn your back while they hold their cards so that everyone can see them. Meanwhile, of course, you change the pack for an ordinary one minus the three cards in question, which you then hand to the persons so that they may return their cards. Of course, this is not as good as forcing three cards in an artistic way, but it is a very good substitute.

Freezing Ice in the Hand

By Long Tack Sam

This is a favorite trick of Chinese magicians and is very old, though, I believe, entirely unknown to the performers of other countries. The effect depends upon the trick being workd neatly and upon the assurance of the magician, but this is very largely true, of course, of every bit of magic either Occidental or Oriental. The Chinese magician is taught while an apprentice to learn the routine and patter of a trick thoroughly and not to vary its performance. Unless every move is the result of studied effort the trick cannot have its full effect. With a bow to Lu Tsu Bing, the patron saint of the Chinese magician, I begin.

The effect is good not only because it is mystifying, but also because it is surprising. From a bowl filled with water, the magician dips out a handful and changes the water into a small block of ice. The hottest weather and the most iceless small town are no hindrance.

The ice is made from a heavy colorless piece of plate glass, chipped to look like an ice block. It should be about an inch and a quarter thick, and must have no sharp edges, so that it can be palmed like a billiard ball.

In performing the trick, the magician has a bowl of water on a small table behind which he stands. Any small opaque bowl will do. The ice is palmed in his right hand. He shows the left hand empty and pulls up the right sleeve. Chinese sleeves have tight cuffs. The sleeves are pulled up, in effect to keep them out of the water, but in reality as a means of showing the hands empty. The left hand is again shown empty after the sleeve is pulled up and the ice, by a change-over palm, is transferred to the left hand. The right hand is shown empty and the left sleeve is pulled up. All this is done without any apparent trickery, the purpose seems to be to keep the sleeves dry, and it is done with slow enough motions so that the audience will not suspect that either hand holds anything.

The left hand is now palming the ice. The right hand is cupped and dipped into the water. A handful is brought out with a flourish, then poured back into the bowl. This should be done to make as big a show as possible of the quantity of water you dip up. This is done several times. Finally the motion of dipping is repeated, but no water is taken up. This time the "water" is apparently poured into the other hand. The left hand is closed around the ice and held thumb up so that the water seemingly goes into the hole made by the curved thumb and first finger. Again, apparently, water is poured into the hand. There will be enough water on the right hand from its previous wettings to shake off a few drops after giving the effect of filling the left hand.

The left hand now seemingly squeezes the water so that it forms the ice block and slowly opens to reveal the ice. You must give the effect of the cold ice freezing your hand. To do this put it first on one hand then the other, each time rubbing the fingers of the free hand

over that hand. This should not be overdone. It is well to try this with a piece of real ice to see what you would do naturally. The ice is finally dropped into the bowl of water. The Chinese magician then walks amongst his audience with the bowl so that the ice may be seen. A piece of chipped glass looks like ice at any time, but in the water it may be shown with safety right among the spectators.

As I said before, this is an old effect in China, but it is very effective and audiences like it. It is pretty safe to say a trick found to be effective in one part of the world can be used to advantage in any other part.

Potato Jones

By Horace Goldin

The mise-en-scene of this illusion was built around the wonderful feat of Capt. Jones, of the British Merchant Marine, in running a shipload of potatoes through the blockade to Santander, Spain, during the Spanish War. These potatoes saved thousands of the Spanish civilian population from starving. The captain became a popular hero with the English and was affectionately nicknamed "Potato Jones." As everyone knew of Capt. Jones and his humanitarian exploit, it not only made the illusion timely but of popular interest.

The effect was that Capt. Jones, or rather one of my assistants suitably uniformed and made-up, was caused to disappear after having been buried in a crate of potatoes. The crate was a wooden and wire mesh affair—the frame was made of wood; the sides, wire mesh. It was therefore possible to see right through the crate. Capt. Jones entered the crate by a door at the back, which was then closed so that he looked as if he were standing in a cage. Then a large sack of potatoes was hoisted up above the crate and opened at the bottom. The potatoes fell down, around and above Capt. Jones in the crate, burying him completely. The crate was then hauled aloft by ropes from above. A large tarpaulin was spread out beneath the crate, and the bottom was opened so that the potatoes fell into the cloth, leaving the crate as empty and innocent-looking as it was in the beginning. Capt. Jones came running down the aisle from the back of the audience to its surprise and delight.

The illusion is based on the optical fact that the eye can discern only one wire mesh, though two be used on each side. This second mesh is nearly a foot inside the visible outside mesh. Bracing slats of wood, at least that seems to be their purpose, mask the edges of the inner wire mesh. The top of the space within the inside wire mesh is also covered with the meshed wire. This is formd into a dome, so that when the potatoes are dropped from the sack, they will fill the spaces between the inner and outer meshes. From the front the crate appears to be full of potatoes, actually they are only between the two meshes.

Capt. Jones enters at the back of the crate. The door is put there to mask the fact that there is a double mesh. It is so designed that inner and outer sections swing out together.

When the potatoes come tumbling into the crate from above, Capt. Jones bends his knees and squats down. When the potatoes cover his squatting figure from view, as the rest of the potatoes pour into the crate, the Captain makes his escape through a trap in the bottom of the crate and a similar opening in the stage beneath it. The instant the crate is filled, the suspended potato sack is swung out of the way and ropes are attached by hooks to the four top corners of the crate. The crate is immediately pulled up into the air. Four

DOTTED LINES
INDICATE THE
INNER WIRE MESH

assistants, one at each corner, spread out the tarpaulin, and a string is pulled which opens the bottom of the suspended crate and releases the potatoes. The bottom of the crate is hinged on the side away from the audience and the potatoes come tumbling down in full view. The crate is empty—the Captain appears in the audience.

The potatoes used in the illusion are artificial. Not only are they lighter than real ones but they can be used over and over again.

The Mysterious Lemon Trick

By Alexander, "The Man Who Knows"

Have a metal card box in your left vest pocket with one cigarette in the top partition so as to give it the appearance of a cigarette case. Have a deck of forcing cards in your right coat pocket. Tear a corner, about three-fourths of an inch square, from one of the force cards. Put this in your right trouser pocket. Fold the rest of the card crosswise until it is about the size of a lead pencil. Push a knife into the end of a lemon until it almost goes out the other end. Force the folded card into this slit and, once the card is inside, squeeze the slit together. If you do this carefully the cut will not be visible at a two-foot distance. You will also need an unprepared lemon. You are now ready to perform.

"Friends, I will present to you a seeming miracle in modern magic. Your attention is called to two lemons, which I would like you to examine. (Toss out the unprepared lemon; hold the other in your left hand. Ask for the examined lemon to be returned, catch it in your right hand. Pretend to exchange it for the lemon in your left hand and again toss out the unprepared lemon. When it is returned, continue with your patter.)

"I have here two unprepared lemons; they have been thoroughly examined. Will someone kindly suggest which one I shall use in this experiment? (If the prepared one is selected, explain that you have no use for the other one, but will use the one of their choice. If the unprepared one is selected, toss it out, remarking that it now belongs to the person who selected it and that you will use the remaining lemon for the feat.)

Borrow a handkerchief and fasten the corners together. Give the lemon to a small boy, have him put it into the handkerchief bag and hold it high at all times.

Spread your forcing deck ribbonwise face down on a tray and allow a lady to freely choose one card. Drop the pack back in your pocket, taking care that the audience cannot see the faces of the cards.

Request the lady to tear the card in two lengthwise, then squarely in two crosswise. Meanwhile, you secretly palm the corner that fits the card in the lemon in your right fingers. Reach for her torn card. Tear the pieces again. Ask her to retain a piece. Pass her the corner which you had finger-palmed.

Get another small boy to assist. Give him the torn pieces. Take out your "cigarette case," remove the single cigarette, which has held the case properly open all the while in your pocket. Tell the boy to drop his pieces into the case. Snap it shut and pass it to him to hold over his head.

"Boys, the secret of this entire experiment lies in two magic words. When I snap my fingers, I want the boy who is holding the case to say 'Opus.' As he does, I desire the other boy, who is holding the lemon in the handkerchief to speak the word 'Pejensus.' If these words are spoken in a low tone of voice, they will cause the pieces of the card to be restored to their natural order, to dematerialize and fade away from the box and become implanted on the inside of this lemon."

Snap your fingers. Take the card case and show it empty. Now remove the lemon from the handkerchief. Slice off the end opposite to that in which the card was inserted. Take out the card, allow the boy to dry it with the handkerchief. Pass it to the lady so that she may fit the corner which she holds.

This I have found to be, beyond a doubt, the most effective lemon trick I know. There are too many angles for them to watch, and you are the master of the situation at all times. A great deal of comedy can be worked up with the boys in saying the magic words.

Baffles' Novel Production Ball Fake

By Charles R. Brush

In the one to four billiard ball trick at the conclusion of the four ball production in the right hand, the performer suddenly reaches out with his left hand and four balls appear there too.

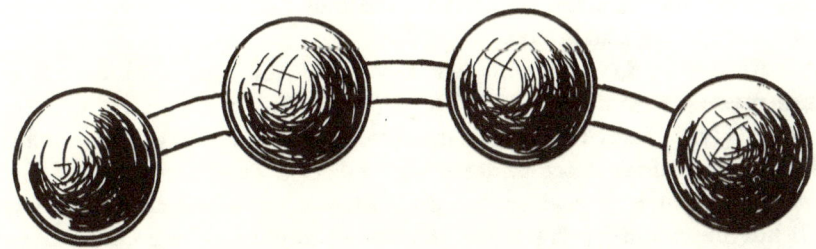

The fake pictured here is perfect for this effect. The four balls are joined together by three flesh-colored strips. A small hook is soldered on the middle strip, which permits the fake to be hung under your coat.

The fake fits exactly between your fingers so there will be no need for quick adjustment when you reach for it. Your fingers dart under your coat, grasp the fake firmly and pull it instantly into view. This is done under cover of the production of the fourth ball in your right hand. The misdirection is excellent.

The Oracle

By David T. Bamberg (Fu Manchu)

Here is a little card trick which I have used myself to great advantage on occasions. It is a particularly good little affair to start things going. You remark about something that happened to you and say: "I knew that was going to happen because I saw it in the cards when I read my fortune last night."

Now this never fails because the girls almost jump down your throat: "Can you tell fortunes in the cards?" And they beg you to read the cards . . . and from then on it's plain sailing; the ice is broken.

The effect of the trick is as follows: You look at a girl and remove a Queen from the pack. If she has black hair, the Queen of Spades; chestnut hair, clubs; blond, hearts; and ash-blonde or platinum, diamonds. Now go through the pack and explain the meaning of various cards in this fashion:

Nine of Hearts is the fulfillment of a wish, the wishing card. The Ten of Clubs is a water journey. The Nine of Clubs a land journey. The Ten of Diamonds, riches. Seven of Clubs, marriage. Ten of Spades, disappointment. The Ace of Spades, death. Three Queens together, scandal. Three Jacks, a fight. Three Kings, good business. There are many other things, but there are books about it and you can find your own combination. The Seven of Hearts is a kiss. The cards are shuffled, then you tell the fortune of the young lady who has selected a card, which is shuffled into the pack. The pack is turned face down on the palm of the left hand and dealt face-up on the table as shown in the illustration.

As the cards are dealt, you say: "An Ace and a Three. Does that mean anything to you? No?" (Deal one card under the upper two, a Five. Deal four more, an Ace, a Nine, a Three and another Nine. Then three more under those, a Ten, a Two and a four. Then one card, which represents the girl.) Stop, point to the cards and say: "It has been told by the cards, that (point to the first two cards, upper row) on the 13th day of the fifth month, May (point to the Five 1-9-3-9, nineteen hundred and thirty-nine (use the date of your performance) at exactly (point to the three card row) 10:24 by the clock, that you (point to the Queen) will be (turn over the next card, the selected card—the Seven of Hearts) kissed by (turn over the last card, a Jack, fair or light as the case may be) a dark young man. Permit me." And you kiss the young lady (on the hand, if you are in doubt). And her fortune is told.

This always gets a big hand. It's really very fine and although

it is not a very subtle trick, it is marvelous for breaking the ice and getting on good terms with everyone and holding their interest.

Now, I have two methods to do this trick. Sometimes I have the cards already stacked except for the hour and minute row, and while I select the cards to explain their meaning in telling fortunes, I give myself about four or five minutes and set the "three row," while showing the cards. I use a blank card should the minute be zero. For the

20th of May I use two Tens. For the 21st, I use a Two-spot and an Ace. Don't use pictures to represent 11, 12, etc. Use two Aces, etc. I use a short Jack of Clubs as a key card. I have the Queen above it with the Seven of Hearts, which must be forced. The shuffling is faked with a lot of loose talk about gipsies and so forth. As this is not presented as a card trick, they suspect nothing and you can get away with murder. I have had some lovely kisses.

The second method is to stack a borrowed pack as you go through it explaining the meaning of the cards.

Neato Silk

By Paul Rosini

The magician causes a silk handkerchief to disappear from his hands and to reappear in a glass some distance away. In basic effect the trick is not new, but in detail it is new and it is a complete novelty to audiences. It is a trick that can be done effectively under any conditions.

The magician shows a piece of paper about nine inches square, and forms it into a cornucopia. The pointed end is folded over several times so that it will not unroll. He uses this to cover an empty stemmed water glass. He puts the glass on a table and picks up a silk handkerchief.

The magician rolls the silk between his hands and apparently leaves it in his left hand. He reaches down with his right hand and plucks the silk from behind his right knee. The left hand is empty. He says: "I will repeat this so that you will have a better opportunity to see it." He again apparently leaves it in his left hand, but this time—not a silk—but a lighted match is produced from behind the knee. His left hand is empty. He touches the match to the cornucopia, which covers the glass. It disappears in a burst of flame, and the handkerchief is seen in the glass.

The cornucopia is made of flash paper. A small strip of flash paper is pasted to one end of the flash paper square from which the cone is made. The duplicate silk is folded by laying it flat and bringing the corners to the center, and continuing to do this until you have a small, compact bundle. This is put on the flashpaper strip, which is rolled around it, then pasted back on the square (see illustration). This permits the handkerchief to be bent back beyond the corner of the paper, so that by holding it, masked in the hand, both sides of the paper may be shown.

Once the cone is made, the point is bent several times to keep it from opening out. The cornucopia is then dropped over the glass.

The magician rolls his silk between his palms; he pretends to take it in his left hand, but keeps it in his right. He produces it from behind his right knee. The second time, the magician keeps the silk in his

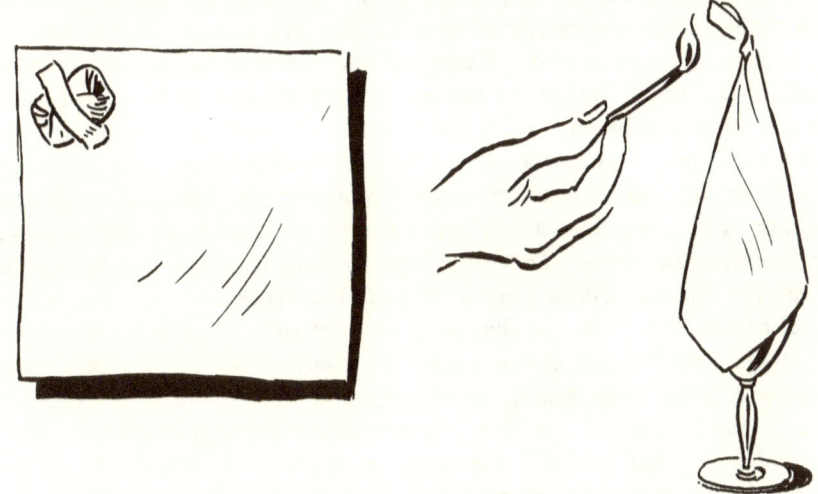

right hand and pulls the match through a tiny hole in the seam of his trousers, where the end protrudes. A match-lighting gimmick such as dealers sell is fastened inside the trouser leg. The withdrawal of the match lights it automatically. The flame is such a surprise that it masks the fact that the closed right hand still holds the silk. The extra silk can be disposed of in one of your pockets when the duplicate is pulled from the glass.

This is the first time that I have ever described a trick for publication. I sincerely hope it appeals to you.

The Imaginary Rubber Band

By Nate Leipzig

There is nothing so entertaining and mystifying as an impromptu trick. One where the magician borrows an article and immediately, without preparation, performs a very fine effect. Such a trick is also valuable for it creates a bigger impression in the minds of newspaper men and club chairmen than a more formal trick. Such an effect I shall now describe.

You commence by borrowing a derby hat and handkerchief. Laying the handkerchief on the table, you take the hat in your left hand. "There is something in a derby hat that not one person in a hundred knows about. It is a very fine, but extremely strong, rubber band, which stretches across the inside of the crown of the hat. Because of its color and fineness, it is almost invisible to the eye. I shall see if I can show it to you." With your left hand still holding the hat, get the nail of any finger of that hand under the hat. With the right hand apparently search for the imaginary elastic, which, at last, you seem to find. Carry out the misdirection by apparently pulling the elastic out of the hat and letting it snap back. The sound of the snap is caused by the finger nail of the left finger against the ribbon. If this is properly carried out, the illusion is perfect.

Now lay the hat on the table and explain that, although the rubber is so very fine, it has great elastic qualities and you propose to demonstrate them. Take the handkerchief and roll it into a ball. Tuck the ends in with a pencil. Put the handkerchief into your inside coat pocket, which is, usually, on your right side. Leave the handkerchief as near the top of the pocket as it will stay. Next pick up the hat with your right hand, apparently find the elastic with your left hand and make believe that you are stretching it toward the handkerchief in your pocket. Carefully carry out the illusion by going through the motions with your hand. Explain that you are looping the rubber around the handkerchief. While you are doing this, your right hand, which is still holding the hat, is held at arm's length.

Next press the elbow of your right arm against the outside of your coat so as to continue the illusion that the rubber is tightly stretched, and that it must be held to keep it from snapping back. The moment the elbow is pressed against the coat, the left hand, with the handkerchief palmed, comes out of the pocket toward the hat. As you reach the hat, squeeze the handkerchief in between the hat and the brim, where it can be wedged tightly enough to stay. Your left hand is now free to show the inside of the hat, and then, in showing the outside, you release the handkerchief with the right hand and turn the hat over so that the handkerchief is brought inside the hat, where it is dropped. In doing this, undo the twist so that the handkerchief will expand.

Take the hat in your left hand and hold it mouth toward the ceiling so that the handkerchief will not show. You are still pressing the right elbow against the right side. Pivot your right hand away from the hat. You are now in the same position as you were when you first made the rubber "snap."

Extend the left hand as far as you can reach, which apparently stretches the rubber to its limit. At that moment lift your right elbow, snap the hat band, turn the hat over and let the handkerchief fall out. This must be done in one move. The whole thing depends upon the mise-en-scene. It must be carried out slowly and evenly. Everything depends on convincing the audience that a rubber band is used.

The method of snapping the rubber is up to you. I prefer snapping the hat band with my finger nail, though you may flick your finger against the side of the hat, or even have a rubber band around the hat. The only trouble with snapping your finger against the hat is that if you don't get the right sound you will not be apt to carry out the illusion.

This trick has perfectly natural moves. There are a lot of good tricks that I never touch for some of the moves in them are not natural. The things one tells an audience must be plausible, or again I will not do the effect. After all, in a trick everything is secondary to the presentation. Always remember—magic is only magic when you completely deceive.

The Self-Extricating Card

By Houdini

"Please be so kind as to select, by name, any card in the pack. I shall run through the pack and find that card. Ah! Here it is. In order that you may be certain that you can hold on to it, please take this wooden pencil and push it right through the card. Thank you. It is, of course, obvious that the only way to free the card from the pencil is to remove it like this. Now, please push the pencil back through

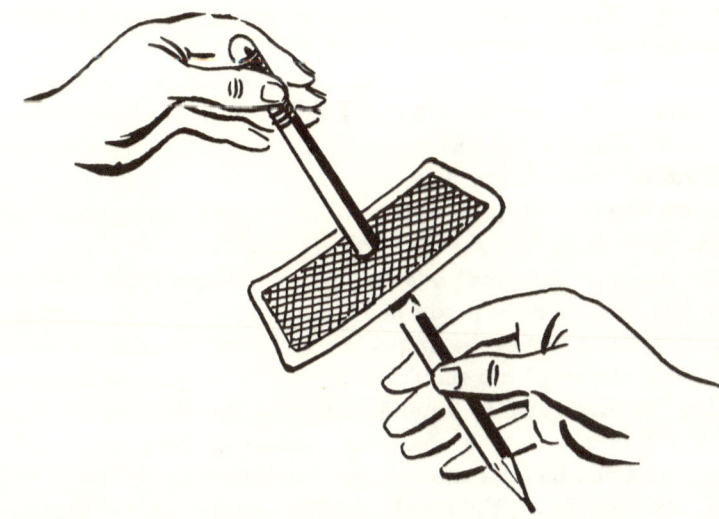

the hole in the card and hold the pencil with the right hand below the card and the left hand above. Hocus Pocus! And the card has escaped from the pencil and here it is in the middle of the pack. You see you hold quite a different card."

The method is really as simple as the trick is effective. When the card is named, take it and the card immediately above it from the pack and hold the two cards as one. Have the pencil pushed through both cards. An excuse is given in the patter to take the card off the pencil. In his left hand, at this point, the magician has the pack, which he puts under the two cards. He then grasps the cards between the pack and his thumb. The pencil he holds in the right hand. When the pencil is returned to the spectator, the left thumb brings the two cards square on top of the pack. The right hand then takes from the pack but one card, and as the spectator sees the hole he has just made in the card, he does not realize the substitution. All that is left to do is to make a pass to bring the selected card to the center of the pack. It adds an amusing touch if the second card used is the Joker.

Yank-A-Hank

By Ross Bertram

A handkerchief is spread out on the table and a quarter is laid on it at the center. The four corners of the handkerchief are then folded in to the center. The performer grasps the top or outermost corner, and shakes out the handkerchief. The quarter has vanished. He then twirls the handkerchief into a rope and ties a knot in it at the middle. The handkerchief is handed to a spectator who finds the quarter securely tied inside the knot.

Method: The familiar wax pellet is not used. This method is entirely impromptu. It is most easily performed on a table covered with a cloth, though a method will be explained for doing the trick on any surface. It is most effective when the spectators are standing, partly because then they can see the coin up until the moment it is covered, partly because the angles are more favorable to the performer. Failing this, the magician should work with his left side to the audience.

The handkerchief is spread out with the right corner hanging over the side of the table, and the quarter at the center. The right hand grasps the inside corner of the handkerchief, fingers above and thumb below. The right hand folds the corner of the handkerchief in just past the center covering the coin and turning palm upward at the same time. The left hand, almost simultaneously, folds its corner in also.

As soon as the right hand is hidden, its first and second fingers open. The second finger presses down on the edge of the quarter nearest the performer, tilting the coin up slightly. The index finger closes in, lifting up the outer edge of the coin, with the result that the coin is flipped on the back of the hand between the first and second fingers.

The right hand now goes to the right corner of the handkerchief. As this is hanging over the side of the table, the hand can grasp it while remaining palm up. At the same time, the left hand picks up

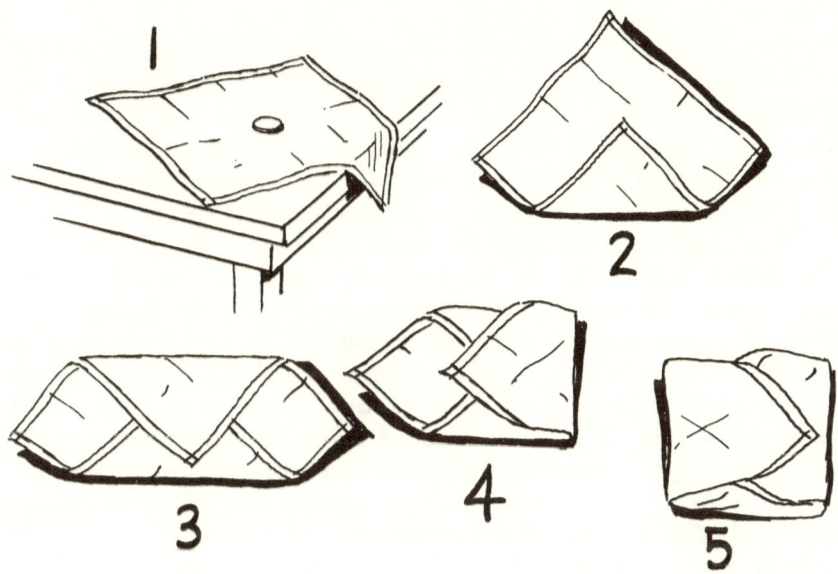

the left corner. The right hand, without turning over, folds its corner in, followed instantly by the left hand. Both hands are dropped to the sides for a moment, and the right thumb pulls the coin to the front of the hand, where it is again clipped between the first and second fingers.

The left hand now picks up the outermost corner and shakes the handkerchief, demonstrating that the coin has vanished. The right hand then takes a corner of the handkerchief and the cloth is shown on both sides.

The right hand moves to take the corner diagonally opposite the left hand. Then follows the familiar business of twirling the handkerchief into a loose rope, thus forming a tube, down which the coin slides into the middle of the twisted handkerchief, where the handkerchief is then knotted with an overhand knot.

To perform the first part of the trick on a hard surface, use a freshly laundered handkerchief and take advantage of the ridge formed by the fold. Let the quarter overlap this ridge so that one side of the coin is raised slightly, ready to be clipped between the fingers.

A Useful "Number" Trick

By Edward Victor

Borrowing a pack of cards, the conjurer asks anybody in the room to think of any card. This person is handed the pack, he is requested to note and remember at what number his card stands from the bottom of the pack. In other words he counts the cards face upward in his hands until he comes to the thought-of card, and notes its number. He is now asked to cut the pack several times.

The magician takes back the cards, gives them a further cut and places them behind his back for a second, immediately returning them to the assistant saying that he has discovered the card. He remarks: "Don't tell me the name of your card, but just say at what number it was from the bottom of the pack." If, for example, the assistant replies "Thirty-seven," the conjurer says: "That's funny! I have altered it to the forty-fourth." This is duly verified by the assistant himself.

Method: First borrow a pack and secretly bend the right hand top corner of the second card from the top slightly inwards. The easiest way to do this is to bend the right hand top corner of the bottom card with the left forefinger and then, gripping the top and bottom cards firmly between the left thumb and fingers, pull away the rest of the pack and put it below them. This brings the bent card into position second from the top. Have a card mentally selected and hand the pack to the thinker face downward, requesting him to ascertain at what number his card lies from the bottom of the pack. The bent corner of the second card is quite invisible as he takes the pack, as it is covered by the top card.

Having found the number his card occupies, the assistant is asked to cut the pack several times — ordinary single cuts, each one completed.

On receiving the cards back, you bring them to their original order by cutting the pack one above the bent, or crimped, card. Placing the pack behind your back for a moment, quickly transfer seven cards from the top of the pack to the bottom. Return the pack to the assistant and inquire the number his card originally occupied. The final position of his card will be seven higher than the number he tells you.

Rope Decapitation

By Ishida Tenkai

The advantage of this version of the rope through neck effect is the apparent fairness of the method. A rope as long as the distance between the magician's fingertips, when his arms are outstretched, is used. The rope is put around the perform's neck and allowed

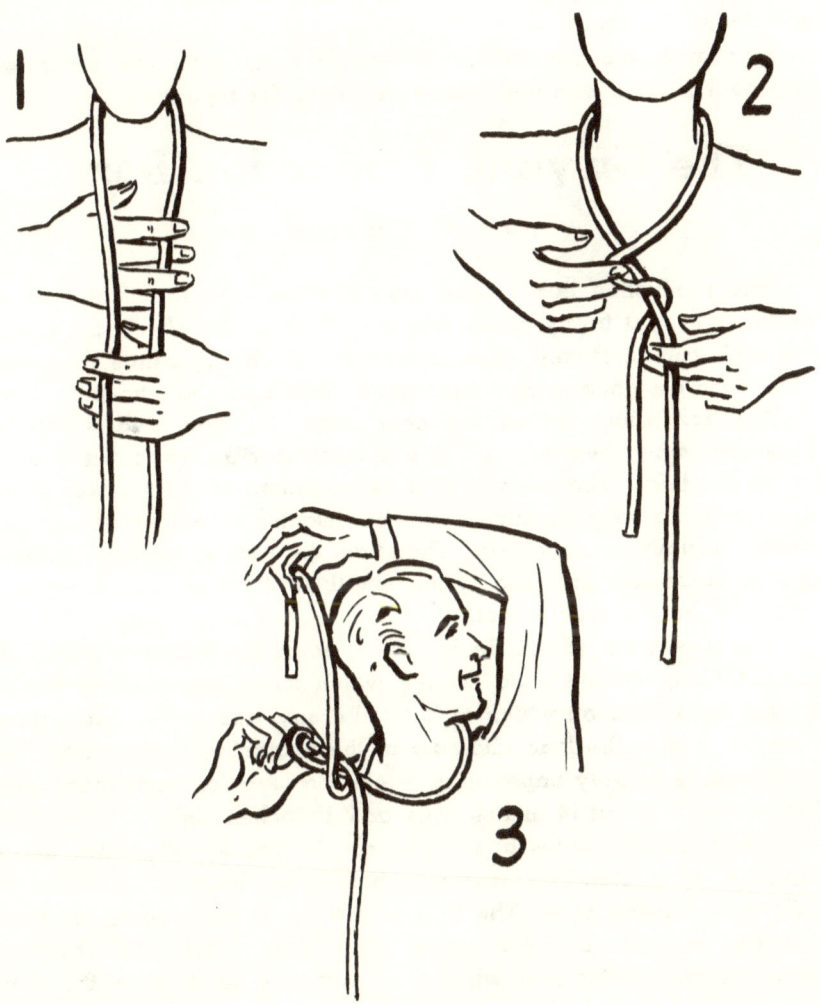

to hang loosely in front. It is then given another turn around the neck and the ends are pulled. The rope appparently passes through the neck and comes free.

The manipulation is in the second twist. There are three parts, which are clearly shown in the accompanying illustration. In the first move, the magician catches hold of the left end of the rope between the first three fingers of his right hand. With his left hand he grasps the right strand between his left first and second fingers.

In the second move, a loop of the left strand is drawn over to the magician's right. While this loop is still held with the left hand, the performer draws the right hand end around his neck. In doing this the left hand, holding the loop, also moves up apparently merely to keep the rope in place. The third figure is exaggerated to better show the manipulation.

As soon as the two ends hang down in front again, the performer takes hold of them with both hands and pulls the rope free.

The Gwynne Production Box

By Jack Gwynne

This production box proved both effective and practical during the time I used it in my vaudeville act. It gives the effect of a large trick with comparatively little apparatus. Such apparatus as there is has been designed to pack in a small place to aid in transportation.

The box, which is built up one panel at a time and which is obviously empty, becomes full of live stock or silks without any suspicious loading. The method is a development of the tip-over principle. It is cleverly disguised and the disguise eliminates the angle problem usually encountered. Therefore, the trick is not only adaptable to stage use but also to the small platform so frequently encountered by the club performer.

The illustration shows, in Figure A, what the audience sees. A small, folding, three-winged screen, which looks like a fancy table, is used as a base on which to build the box, and at the same time it serves to hide the load chamber at the beginning of the trick. As this screen is entirely unprepared, it can be used for many purposes. Each panel is about 14 inches wide and 32 inches high.

The back and sides of the box are hinged to fall down, as in Figure A, or to stand up to form a box as in Figure B. The box is built on a wooden tray. The front of the box is fastened to the load chamber and draws it into place. One side of the load chamber forms the front of the box, while the lower side, as it fits in the tray, forms the bottom of the box.

Figure E shows the shape and construction of the load chamber. This is pivoted to the tray so as to hang down inside the screen until the box is built. It is pulled into place in the box when the front panel is drawn up.

To prepare the trick, the box must be set up on the screen as in Figure D. The chamber is loaded and put out of sight by folding

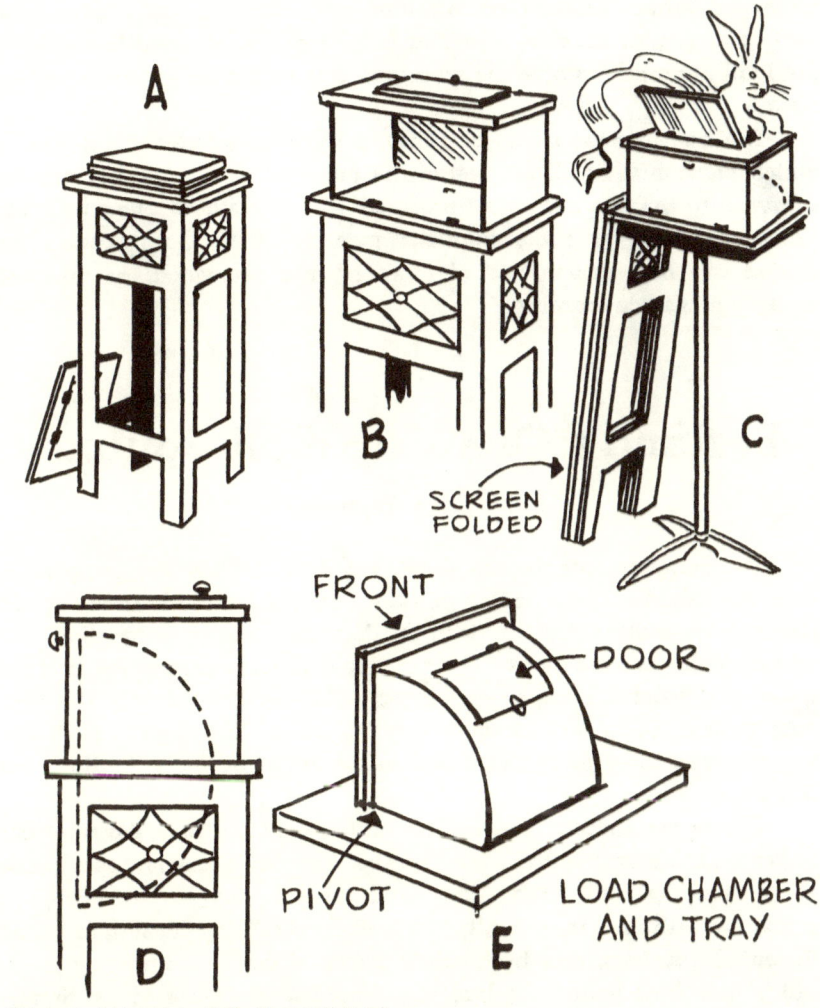

SIDE VIEW OF SCREEN

down the front to lower the chamber inside the screen. The box is then taken apart, and folded as in Figure A. The top cover is stood on the floor and leaned against the screen.

In presenting the trick, the performer stands behind the screen and calls attention to the folded box. The back and two sides are raised and the lid is put on. The box then appears as in Figure B. Attention is called to the emptiness of the box, and the front is raised to bring the load chamber into the box.

The front has a leather tab, or small metal ring, fastened to it, so that the performer may catch hold of it with ease. The tray, with the box built upon it, is removed from the screen and placed on an undraped table. The screen is folded and casually laid aside. The performer is now able, by opening the lid of the box and the door in the load chamber, to produce whatever it was that he carefully tucked away.

The box may be made of polished wood or painted a solid color which harmonizes with the rest of the material in the act, or both the screen and the box may be decorated with a Chinese or some other Oriental design or some futuristic pattern. Both the box and the screen are best constructed of three or five ply wood, as this will entirely eliminate warping.

Berland's One Cup Ball Routine

By Sam Berland

The requirements for the One Cup Ball Routine are simple. A common drinking glass (fooled you already; it's not really a cup at all), two rubber balls about an inch in diameter, and a large ball that will fit easily into the glass. Form a piece of paper around the inverted glass and twist the paper at the top. All the balls are in the right coat pocket. You will need to learn to make a "pass." A "pass" wherein you apparently put a ball in the left hand but actually retain it in the right.

This is the simplest pass. The ball is held between the right first finger and the ball of the right thumb. The left hand is open, ready to receive the ball. The right hand turns to the left as though to place the ball therein, actually the ball is rolled by the thumb across the middle fingers, and by a slight curve of the little finger, plus the aid of the third finger, the ball is retained at the base of the fingers. The left hand closes, apparently over the ball. The ball is easily held in the right hand with but little pressure. Practice until you can hold your right hand relaxed, without any suggestion of strain, as you hold the concealed ball.

To "load" the ball into the covered glass, hold the ball as explained at the base of the little finger. Now put your hand around the glass, thumb on one side, fingers on the other. The fingers and thumb rest on the table, hugging the glass. Lift the glass about three or four inches from the table. Allow it to tilt forward slightly. Move the little and third fingers, which hold the ball, slightly inward. If

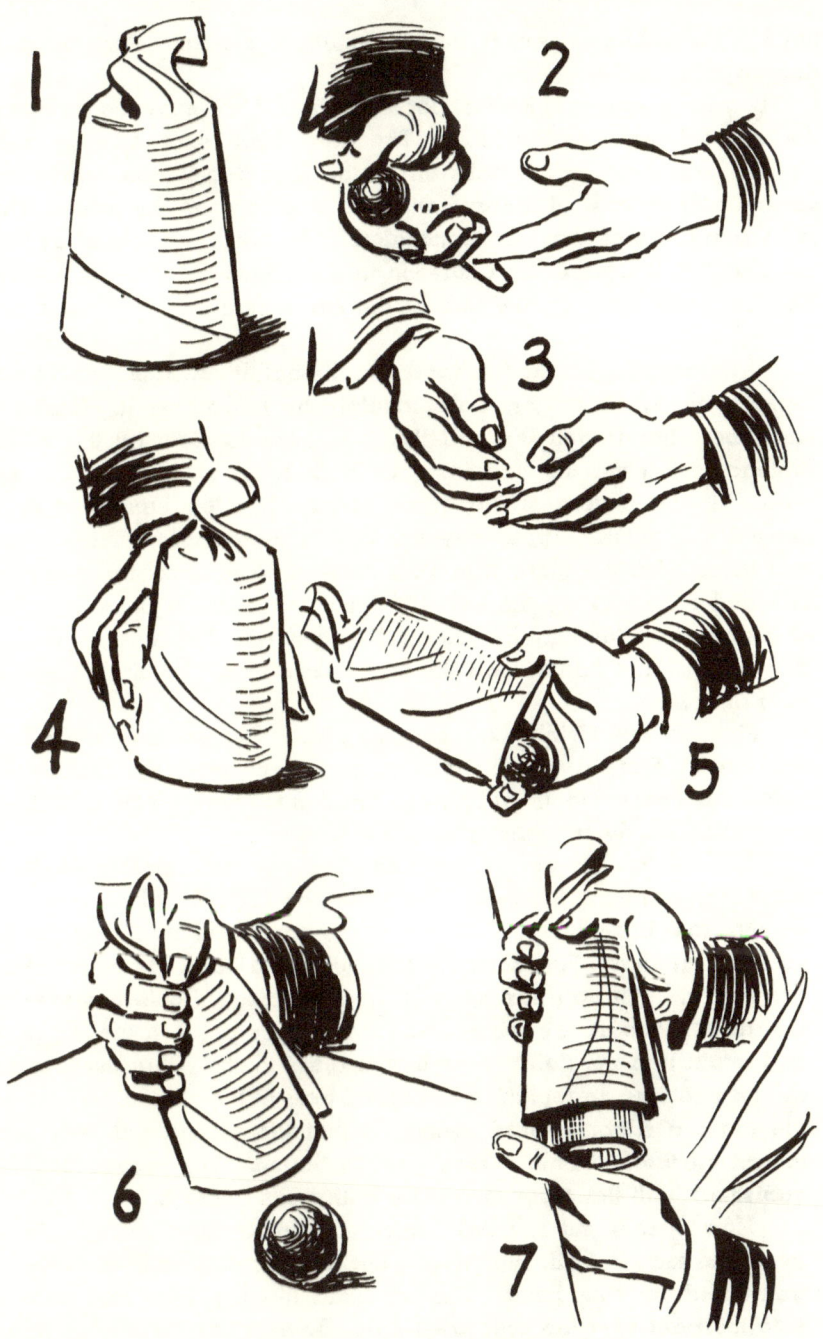

you lower the glass and release the ball, it will go under the glass without hesitation.

You have learned the "pass" and the "load," and with all the balls in the right coat pocket, you are ready to perform. Perform on a draped table.

Borrow a glass, twist the paper around it as explained. Place the inverted glass on the table. The right hand reaches in the coat pocket, palms one of the balls under the little finger, and brings the second ball in view of the audience. It is placed on the table. The right hand, which has the concealed ball, takes the glass by the top and lifts it toward the audience to show that the glass is empty. The left hand picks up the ball at the same time the right hand lifts the glass.

With attention on the left hand and the ball it holds, the right hand replaces the glass on the table, loading the ball under it. Casually show both hands and the ball that has been in view all the while. Pretend to transfer the ball from the right hand to the left. Use the pass. Tit the bottom of the glass, holding the left hand flat as it touches the glass. Apparently the ball is driven through the paper and glass. Lift the glass with your right hand to show the duplicate ball under it. Pick up the ball with your left hand, replace the glass with your right, loading the other ball as you do. Repeat this passing-through feat, but do not load the cup a third time. Retain the ball in your right hand.

Pick up the visible ball on the table. Remark that there is a wart on it. Pretend to pull the wart away, and bring the ball, which has been concealed in your right hand into view. You now have two balls. Put them on the table.

Apparently put one of the balls in your left hand, retain it in the right by making the pass. The right hand lifts the glass to show it empty, and, in replacing it, loads in the concealed ball. Hit the left hand on the glass, then show that the left hand—and the right hand—are empty. The ball has apparently penetrated. Don't, however, lift the glass. Pick up the second ball, apparently put it in the left hand, and retain it in the right. Now lift the glass to show that the first ball did go through. In replacing the glass, load in the second ball, giving the glass a slight upward sweep so that the second ball will come to rest on the first ball. Open your left hand. The second ball has vanished! Lift the glass and show both balls under it.

Now openly put one ball under the glass. Say that you do not need the second ball. Put it in your pocket, but palm it out when you withdraw your hand. The left hand lifts the glass and transfers it to the right over the concealed ball. Then it lifts the visible ball to the table. The right hand replaces the glass with the other ball under it. The left hand openly passes its ball to the right hand. The right hand apparently puts it in the pocket, again retaining it. Once more the above described move is repeated.

Finally the right hand, in going to the pocket, drops the small ball and palms out the large ball. The left hand places the glass over the right hand as before, and the large ball is loaded when the right hand puts the glass on the table. Put the visible small ball in your right pocket.

Ask someone to tap the covered glass to break the spell of the balls appearing.

The left hand is held against the back of the table, meanwhile, with the thumb on the table, the fingers extending downward. The right hand grasps the wrapped glass at the top, thumb and fingers around the twisted end. This is important. Now slowly lift the glass to reveal the large ball. The hand holding the glass moves back to the edge of the table nearest you. Using the appearance of the large ball as misdirection, the right hand lowers the covered glass just slightly below the edge of the table. The hold on the glass through the paper is released. The glass drops secretly out of the paper and onto the fingers of the waiting left hand.

Immediately the right hand moves over the table again. The paper still retains the shape of the glass. Now don't hurry. Congratulate the spectator on breaking the spell. Cover the large ball with the paper shape. Tell the spectator to hit the bottom of the glass again. Imagine his amazement when he does and finds that the glass has vanished. The left hand reaches under the table and brings out the glass.

Here you have an impromptu routine that has all the old features, including the vanishing glass, which was long discarded but is now beautifully revived as a logical and astonishing climax. This is a routine which will appear different to those who are tired of seeing the regular Cups and Balls.

The Vanishing Cigarette

By Jarrow

In some ways a trick is like a joke. For instance, audiences laugh harder at an old joke with a new twist than they do at a brand new joke. The same thing is true in a trick. If the audience thinks it knows what is going to happen, maybe even thinks it knows how it happens, and then is fooled, everyone remembers that trick and talks about it. That is a really good trick.

Do not say to yourself that this trick is old and just a bit different from the one where the magician spreads a handkerchief over one fist, pokes a little pocket in it, drops the lighted cigarette butt inside, then shakes out the handkerchief to show that the butt is gone. Sure it is like it. But, partly because it is like it, and partly because it is different, it is a fine trick. It is the sort of thing that makes an audience gasp.

The magician lights a cigarette, he shows his hands to be empty, then he makes a fist of his left hand. He takes the full length lighted cigarette with his right hand and puts it, lighted end down, into his fist. He takes his right hand away and fans the left fist. Slowly he opens his left hand, the cigarette is gone. Both hands are empty.

Using a bare hand, rather than a handkerchief, makes the trick look better to the audience. The cigarette was vanished in a thumb tip, but how do you get a full length cigarette in an inch long thumb tip? That is the new part of the trick and the part which makes it stand out in the minds of the audience. Not that they know about the thumb tip, but the cigarette is so big it seems impossible to hide — but they saw it vanish.

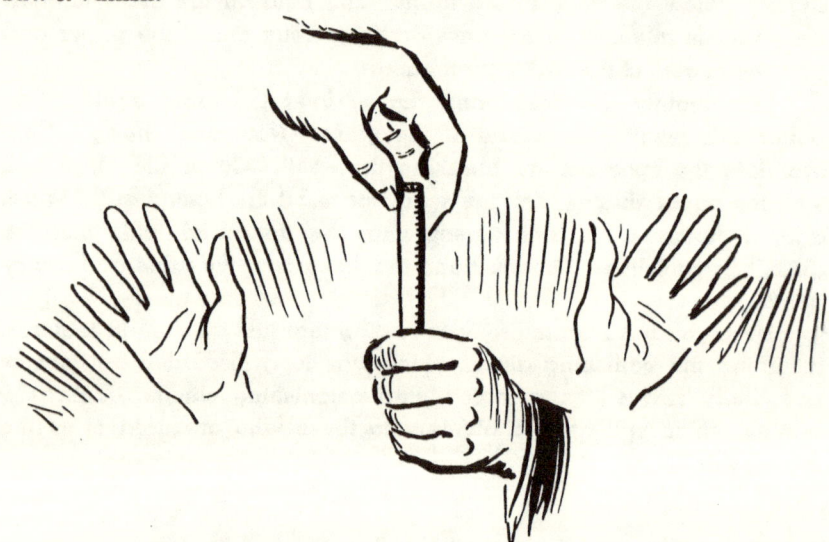

Preparation: Carefully pull the tobacco from one end of a cigarette until only about three-quarters of the tobacco is left. Roll a piece of paper, two inches long and one inch wide, into a tube. Insert this in the open end of the cigarette. The paper should be just a trifle heavier than the cigarette paper. This will make a fake cigarette that can be handled like an ordinary cigarette, but when pushed into a thumb tip will crush up so that it will take but little space.

The best way to take tobacco out of a cigarette is to roll it between your hands and squeeze one end. This will loosen the tobacco so that it will fall out. If you make up several cigarettes at once you will always be prepared to perform the trick. Naturally because of the fire, you must use a metal—not a celluloid—thumb tip.

Put the prepared cigarette in the pack, tobacco end down. You can recognize it immediately. When you are ready to perform put it in your mouth. When you put the cigarette package back in your pocket you steal the thumb tip.

After the vanish, reach into your coat pocket for your handkerchief, wipe your mouth and return the handkerchief to your pocket. When getting the handkerchief leave the thumb tip and all it contains behind in the pocket.

The Time Is

By Herman Yerger

This pocket effect is a very good advertisement because it will be talked about, and your name and address is left in the hands of a spectator.

Should anyone ask you the time, immediately pull out a card and jot down the correct time, which you pass to the questioner. No reference is made to a watch. Apparently you are a human timepiece.

The card I use has "The time is ...." printed on one side and "Next time get Yerger the Magician" with my address under it on the other side.

Now as to method. Several cards are glued together to form a solid block. Imbedded in this block is a wrist watch, minus the strap. The thinner the watch, the better. Several separate cards are on top of the block, thus hiding the watch.

When someone asks the time, I take out the cards, fan them

slightly so that I can secretly glimpse the face of the watch, then I square up the pack and write the time on the uppermost card.

Your ability to "sense" the correct time will be talked about. Further, as the spectator keeps the card, he will be reminded of your feat each time he sees it—and your address for future engagements is on the reverse side.

A Great Production

By Blackstone

This is presented as a Chinese effect. If the performer wears a Chinese hat and robe, it will help the illusion, but the hat alone will suffice. A Chinese walk and a little Chinese talk will help as well. The performer takes a shawl and carefully spreads it out upon the stage (or upon the floor, for this effect can be used for a floor show). pattering all the while. He takes a second shawl, brings it out open until he is right over the one on the stage. He kneels on the first shawl, and, as he rises, whips away the second to disclose a tub, from which shoots up a spray of water and from which jump a couple of ducks. Being ducks, they will stay right under the spray, which shoots out about a foot beyond the tub.

The shawls, or foulards, are sixty inches square and innocent. They should be of different colors and, if possible, Chinese. At the beginning of the trick the shawls are hung, one on top of the other, over the back of a chair. The shawls cover and hide the tub, which hangs from the top of, and behind, the chair.

The drawings of the tub speak for themselves. The tub legs, of three-fourths inch strap iron, are crescent-shaped, with the ends pointed inward. At the top of the tub, at a point on the rim immediately above one of the legs, is the hook by which the tub is hung to the back of the chair.

When the magician picks up each shawl he walks behind the chair and, stooping over, picks up the shawl by the two top corners. The second time this is done as he leans forward he hooks the leg of the tub on his vest or belt. He then walks forward holding the shawl well extended. Kneeling will allow the tub to disengage itself. There is a canvas covering over the tub to hold in the ducks. This has a rope edging. The rope should have a loop on one end to be used as a slip knot to hold the canvas under the wire edge of the tub. A slight pull will release the canvas.

As soon as the tub has been released, as the magician kneels on the stage, he whips off the canvas and reaches in to turn the

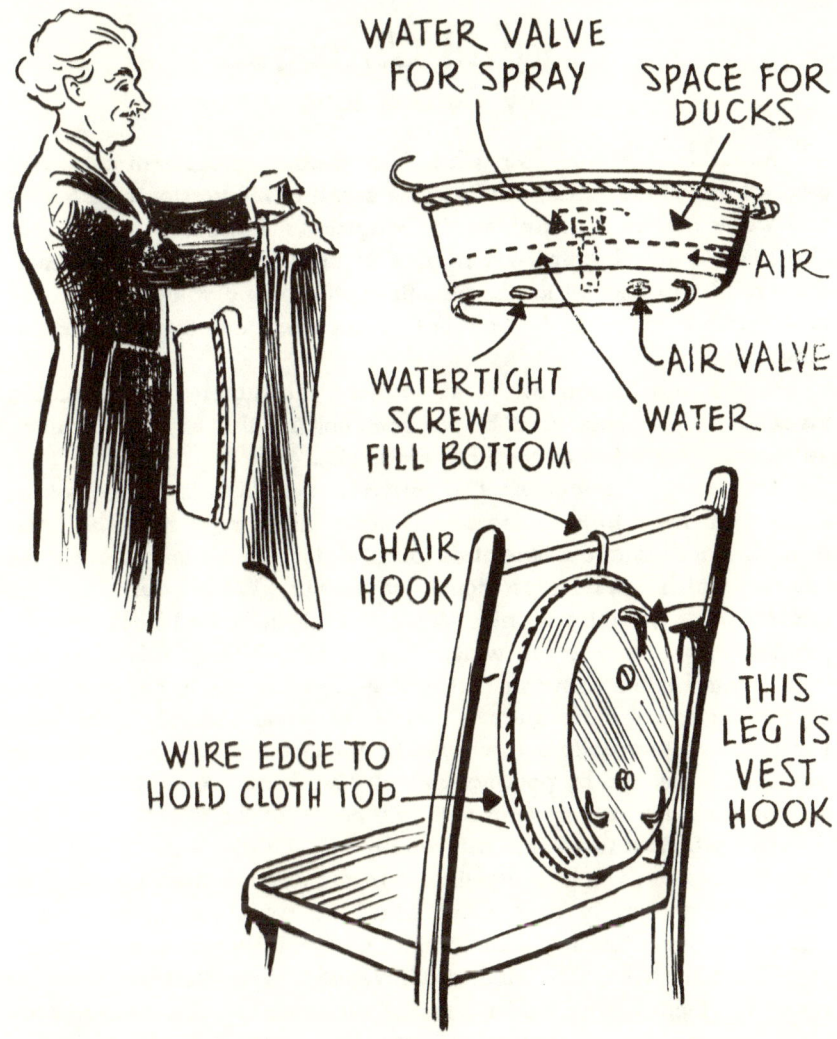

WATER VALVE FOR SPRAY

SPACE FOR DUCKS

AIR

AIR VALVE

WATERTIGHT SCREW TO FILL BOTTOM

WATER

CHAIR HOOK

THIS LEG IS VEST HOOK

WIRE EDGE TO HOLD CLOTH TOP

long handle for the spray effect. The bottom shawl, by the way, will absorb the water which goes outside of the tub.

The illustration shows the compartment for the water and compressed air at the bottom of the tub. Experiment will show the quantity of water to use and the amount of air pressure necessary to produce the best effect. There is a water-tight screw at the bottom of the tub which may be taken out, so that you may put water in the compartment. Also at the bottom is the air valve for the compressed air, which is put in by hand pump. The space between the bottom of the tub and the lower end of the spray pipe should be one-quarter of an inch. There is a long handle on the spray so that you can reach it quickly and turn it on without fumbling during the production.

Liquid Change
By Carlton King

About 1910 or 1911 Mr. Chris Van Bern, a prominent and very original British magician, put forth the secret of his version of the wine and water trick in Will Goldston's "Magician's Annual." I have seen him perform this baffling experiment in his vaudeville entertainment and until he exposed it for the benefit of other wand wielders it proved most puzzling owing to the fact that he used only one tumbler and one glass jug.

At the introduction of the experiment, the tumbler was standing inverted on the table, and before commencing the various changes, he wiped it out thoroughly with a small silk.

The effect is as follows: The performer stands in the center of the stage well away from tables and chairs. In his right hand he holds a small glass jug about two-thirds full of water. In the left he holds the tumbler, which has been previously wiped out. Water poured into the tumbler turns instantly to ink. When the ink is poured back into the jug, the whole turns to red wine. The performer pours this back and forth several times showing that further changes are impossible, then he remarks: "But if I require a tumbler of water I simply pour it out like this." Suiting actions to words, he pours a tumbler of water from the jug of wine, and by pouring the water back into the jug changes the whole into water as it was at first. So much for the effect.

The practical magician will readily see the clean cut effect, also, how it lends itself to comedy lines. In the method used by Mr. Van Bern a very cleverly constructed glass jug was used. Some years ago I was using this jug when, unfortunately, it was broken in transit.

Necessity being the "mother of invention," I devised the following method, which I found works quite as successfully. A glass jug must be procured with a handle of the straight variety. An old-fashioned fountain pen filler, or eye dropper, must also be procured. This is securely fastened, opening downward, to the handle of the jug. A tablespoon full of Salicylate of Soda is dissolved in the water of the jug. Secure a quantity of Double Steel Drops from a drug store. Heat the bottom of the tumbler over a candle flame and paint a minute spot of this preparation on the inside bottom. This will dry quickly and the tumbler may be handled with impunity, even casually examined if desired. The fountain pen filler is charged with a quantity of highly concentrated Oxalic Acid.

Everything is now ready. When the water is poured into the tumbler it instantly changes to ink. When it is poured back into the jug, wine results. This is poured back and forth several times. At

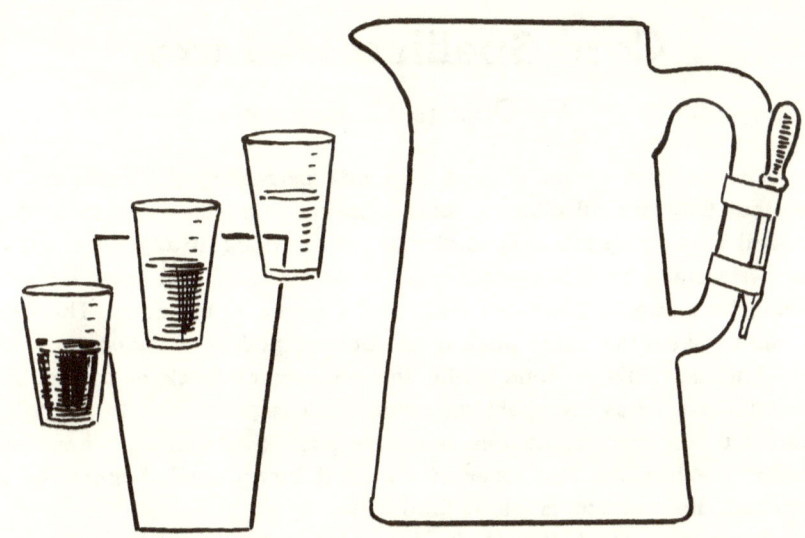

a moment when the tumbler is empty, under cover of misdirecting patter, bring the tumbler under the jug slightly to the rear. The right hand, holding the jug, gives the bulb of the filler a squeeze. This shoots the acid into the tumbler. Thus, when the wine is poured into the tumbler a change to water occurs. This being added to the contents of the jug turns all to water as it was in the beginning.

I would advise care in using the acid — be sure not to get it on your clothes while performing.

Flash Bill Stunt

By Dr. J. G. F. Holston

The following makes a good gag for the new flash bills that are on the market. Dig out from the attic one of those money machines that you put away long ago, or invest in a new one.

As an interlude state that you bought one of these machines from a stranger the other day for only one hundred dollars. You have been running the machine more or less ever since and are thinking of putting an electric motor on it.

While pattering, pick up a piece of blank paper and run it through the machine. Out comes a bill. Have a lighted candle on the table. State that the bill is a lot better than the one printed by the government.

As you are examining it by holding it to the candle, unfortunately you get too close and—puff! It is gone. Remark: "Oh, well, easy come, easy go."

Card Spelling De Luxe

By George G. Kaplan

The performer fans a deck of cards permitting the audience to see that they are all different, and, after allowing the pack to be cut several times, requests a spectator to cut the deck at any point while the performer's back is turned, remove the top card and, after remembering its name, to insert the card in the center of the deck. Then he is told to place the entire pack in the outside pocket of his coat.

Although this is done while the performer's back is turned, he nevertheless takes the spectator's wrist and requests him to mentally spell out his card, using one letter for each card removed from his pocket. When the last letter of the card being spelled mentally is reached, the spectator is told to think "Stop."

In spite of the fact that not a single question is asked, the performer, after removing a number of cards from the spectator's pocket, suddenly calls out: "You just thought of the word 'stop,' did you not? Well, strange to say, I not only received the mental impulse to stop, but the card I am now holding is the one you are thinking of. Will you please name it for the benefit of the audience?" When the card is named the performer displays the card he is holding. It proves to be the thought-of card.

The clean-cut manner in which this effect may be performed from beginning to end will leave a profound effect upon the spectators and, at the same time, should commend itself to the up-to-date performer.

Secret: Although the performer fans the pack and the cards appear to be different, it consists of four series of twelve cards each, arranged as follows:

5 S	K H	Q C	9 H	J S	8 C
3 C	Q H	9 S	4 H	J H	K H

Now, regardless of where the spectator cuts the deck, if he should glance at the top card and replace it in the center of the pack, the twelfth card from the top will always be a duplicate of the one he looked at.

Furthermore, any card that he will think of will have exactly twelve letters, so that although the spectator spells out his card mentally, if the performer counts the cards as they are removed from the pocket until the twelfth appears, this will be the duplicate of the selected card.

The Boudoir of the Dancing Girl

By T. Page Wright and William Larsen

Style of performance in magic is something seldom discussed, but it is vital in the consideration of this particular illusion. A broad comedy presentation or one of heavy mystery would be equally out of place. The illusion must be handled lightly and deftly in a style of high comedy; comedy not in the sense that the magician is working for laughs, but simply that the illusion is presented as divertisement, not to be taken seriously either from the standpoint of effect or mystery. It is in a measure curious that although the gruesome is frequently used as an illusionary background and, occasionally, the broadly spectacular the elements of simple beauty and grace are almost entirely neglected. Yet beauty dwells in smaller things than expensive scenic effects, and grace is an addition to any presentation.

The entire effect not only should be, but absolutely must be done to the accompaniment of music throughout. The whole experiment can be handled better in pantomime than with the aid of speech, and music is essential to the atmosphere.

The illusion is best preceded by a small item which can be done before the front curtain, so that the effect may be discovered ready set. At the conclusion of his minor problem, the magician steps to one side and, as the music starts, motions the front curtain up. Upon the stage a girl is discovered. As the curtain rises she begins to dance. She is young, she is pretty, and she dances well—a light dance utterly free from any suggestion of "jazziness." The stage need not be too brilliantly lit—better that the lights be somewhat dimmed that she may stand out more strongly in contrast in the brilliance of the spotlight. To one side of the stage the magician stands, motionless, as much a spectator for the moment as anyone in the audience

The dance ends, but the music continues through the illusion, though more softly, as a delicate accompaniment. Lightly the girl runs over to where, slightly to one side of the stage, stands her "boudoir." This is a cabinet, without front, decorated inside in light colors as a lady's boudoir might be decorated, and containing for furniture a light dressing table, standing with its back against the back of the cabinet.

The cabinet is raised from the stage a foot or two, so that the audience may see underneath it at all times. Into this the girl steps, still moving in time to the music. She smiles out at the audience, then around at the performer, who has moved across the stage and now stands beside the cabinet. She reaches up and pulls down a spring blind on a roller, like a window curtain, to close the front of the cabinet. As she does, the magician pushes a switch in the side of the cabinet

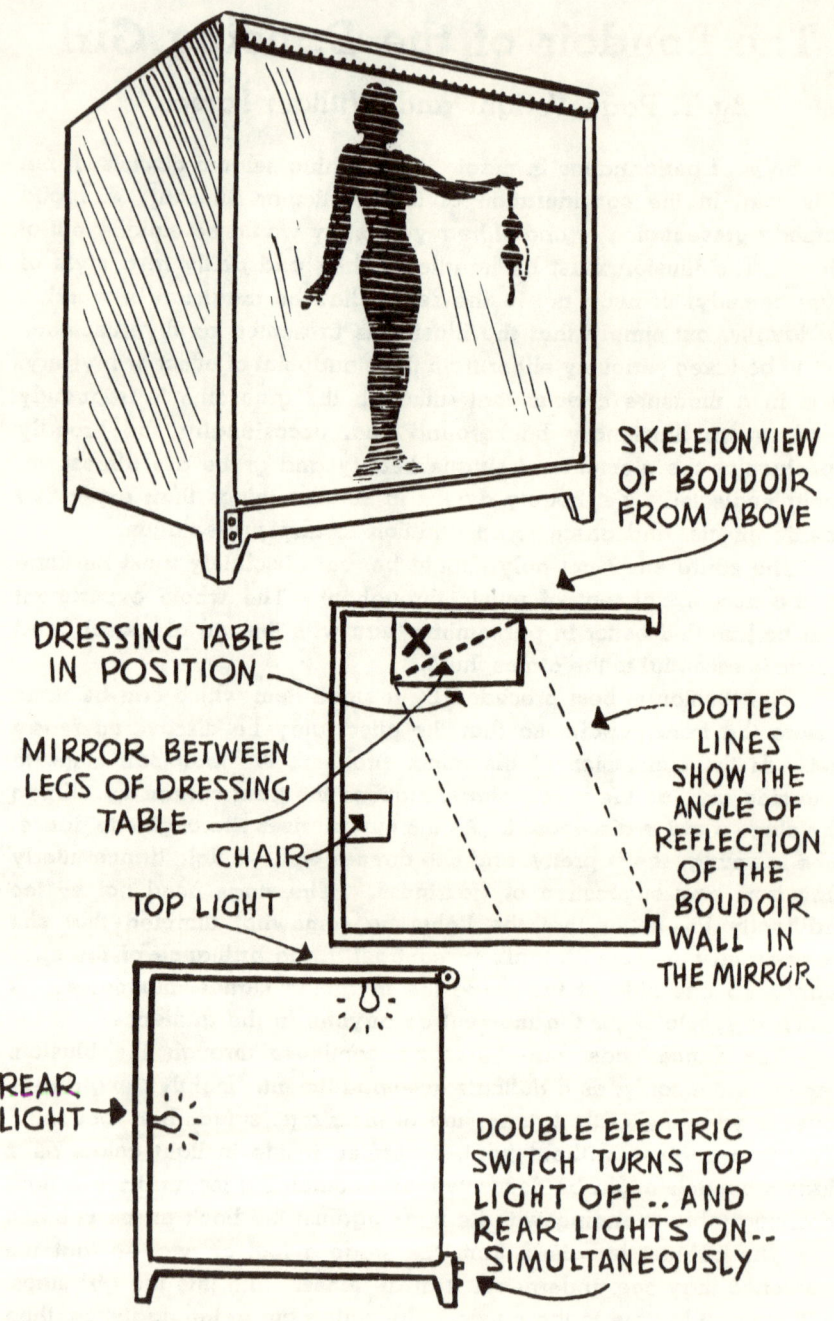

SKELETON VIEW OF BOUDOIR FROM ABOVE

DRESSING TABLE IN POSITION

MIRROR BETWEEN LEGS OF DRESSING TABLE

CHAIR

TOP LIGHT

DOTTED LINES SHOW THE ANGLE OF REFLECTION OF THE BOUDOIR WALL IN THE MIRROR

REAR LIGHT

DOUBLE ELECTRIC SWITCH TURNS TOP LIGHT OFF.. AND REAR LIGHTS ON.. SIMULTANEOUSLY

and a light is switched on, set in the middle of the inside back of the curtain.

She is starting to disrobe; as the audience watches her silhouette form she reaches down and daintily pulls off one slipper, then the other. Then, one at a time, she rolls down her stockings, and slips them off. Next she allows her dress to slip from her and drop upon the floor of the cabinet, and finally her underthings. She stands posed for a moment in shadow. As she does, the magician leans over and takes hold of the bottom of the roller curtain and raises it. But the gasp of the audience dies as it begins, for the shadow has vanished instantly and, as the curtain goes up, it discloses the boudoir empty. Nowhere is there room inside for the girl to be concealed, yet she is not there. The assistants turn the cabinet about. Since the front of the cabinet is open, there can be no question about the matter. Inside and outside are visible at the same time, but the girl is gone.

Though it will be recognized that the instantaneous and almost visible vanishment provides mystery, it is subordinate to the general effect. The whole illusion carries something of the atmosphere of a modern revue. And why not?

We can hardly wish to compete with that form of entertainment entirely, but we may well derive from it what we can in the way of diversion to give variety to our own performance.

But, if this be done, it must be done properly. The girl must be a good dancer, must be dainty and pretty. Costume and setting must be fitting and good looking, and the performer must be able to carry out his part of the performance with grace, playing it as light comedy, yet permitting nothing in his behavior that will give the effect to the whole of vulgarity. Unless it is done thus, the atmosphere will suggest, not a revue, but a cheap burlesque.

Magically, the arrangements are simple. The cabinet is no more than it appears to be. It is fitted, however, with two lights inside, one at the back and the other at the top, near the front. The wiring is so arranged that throwing a switch at the side of the cabinet, on the outside, will switch the current from one light to the other. The two are on a single switch so that the light change will be instantaneous. At the start the top light is on.

During the dance the magician yields the stage entirely to the girl. He stands to one side watching and motionless, for no attention is being paid him anyway. But as the girl finishes and steps into the cabinet, he comes across the stage and stands beside it. As she pulls down the spring blind, he throws the switch so that the top light of the cabinet goes off, and the back light goes on. This he does just as she has the curtain half way down, so that the shadow movements may be followed from the beginning. The light must not be switched on too soon, however, or it would shine directly into the eyes of the audience, and as it must be sufficiently strong to throw a single sharp shadow of the girl upon the shade it would prove most disagreeable.

When the disrobing has been completed the magician leans over and throws the switch again and then deliberately takes hold of the curtain and raises it. The throwing of the switch has, of course, made the shadow invisible since it is the top light which is now on, and as the magician moves deliberately there is a space of about five seconds before the curtain is raised; time enough for a well-rehearsed girl to get safely into her hiding place. But where is her hiding place?

Apparently there is no space where she could be concealed. Actually, however, the innocent-looking and thin dressing table is not what it appears to be. For from the leg toward the audience against the cabinet wall a mirror runs to the leg diagonally opposite, creating a triangular space of just sufficient size to contain the girl. As the only clothing she wears at this time consists of garments stretched flesh-tight about her breasts and hips, the table may be quite small. It is hardly necessary to remark to an audience of magicians that the reflection of the opposite side of the cabinet will appear to be the back of the cabinet seen under the dressing table, and that the reflection of the third leg will appear as the fourth leg. The decoration of the interior of the cabinet as a boudoir, the presence of the chair and general use of the cabinet as a dressing—or rather un-dressing-room— all serve to make the dressing table fit in with the mise-en-scene and a natural furnishing for the cabinet. It might be pointed out that the mirror to be used in this experiment is smaller, and consequently more portable, than in the majority of such self-contained mirror illusions.

It will be obvious that the exact time taken by the girl in getting out of sight must be ascertained by careful rehearsal, for upon her speed depends the effectiveness of the mystery. Any seconds that the magician may waste before raising the curtain once she is out of sight will lesson the efffect of the illusion by that much. For him to raise the curtain even a fraction of a second too soon, on the other hand, would end the performance then and there.

Flowers and Watch

By Ed Reno

This is an effect to follow the effective growth of flowers a la Kellar. The magician has just finished the production of the one red and the one white rose bush. He then holds the cone over his own hand, having no other flower pot, and on lifting the cone discloses a blooming plant in a flower pot. This is a real flower. I always use a geranium which I buy at the dime store. The plant is presented to someone in the audience. Seemingly this is the finale of the effect. I then borrow a watch. Incidentally, although I use a watch and believe it to be more effective, it is quite possible to use a borrowed ring instead. The watch is put in a small box for safekeeping. I then ask the spectator holding the geranium to lift it higher in the air. I fire a pistol and show that the watch has disappeared from the box. Immediately I go to the person holding the plant and pull it up by the roots. Hanging down

STRING AND WATCH SWIVEL HANG BEHIND FLOWER POT

amongst the roots on a string is the watch borrowed just a moment before. This is an effect that the audience can understand as well as appreciate. Not only is it effective, but it is easy to do and what is more important sure-fire. Furthermore, there are no difficulties in its presentation.

It is quite unnecessary to devote space to a description of the method for performing the Kellar Flower Growth, for you all know that. Even if you have forgotten the details, it has been described fully elsewhere and is still sold by several of the dealers. The production of the geranium is merely a continuation of that trick. It may be done after the production of the first rose bush, although I feel it is more effective to "grow" two rose bushes in the customary manner.

The watch is caused to disappear by means of the Watch Box, which is still an excellent trick though infrequently used today. Shooting a pistol at the flower is good business even though it has absolutely nothing to do with the trick.

To the stem of the geranium I have tied, before the performance, a brown string, colored to match the roots. To the other end of this string is fastened a watch swivel-catch. The string should be of such length that after the plant has been pulled from the pot, the end of the string hangs among the roots. When the plant is presented to a spectator, the string hangs over the edge of the flower pot.

The Watch Box, as you know, returns the watch to me. When I go to the person holding the geranium all that is necessary to do is to snap the watch on the swivel-catch, which is easy, and pull out the plant by the roots. The watch appears to be tied to the roots. The string and watch are removed and the watch is returned. The flower is replanted and given back to the spectator.

Before the performance the earth should be softened with a knife or similar instrument so that the plant will pull out easily.

It is not necessary, although I present it that way, to do the Kellar Growth of Flowers first, for the Flower and Watch feat is very effective by itself.

A Tube of Many Mysteries
By Dr. E. G. Ervin

The simple piece of conjuring apparatus presently to be described is capable of infinite variation. It may well be used to produce a silk handkerchief in a glass previously shown empty. Again, a red silk may be placed in the glass, which has been covered with the tube, and a color change to green effected. Or it may be used to advantage in the popular twentieth century handkerchief trick

The tube is of sufficient diameter to permit its being slipped over an ordinary drinking glass. Its length is about six inches. It may be readily constructed out of cardboard. Four small holes are punched in the tube, two on each end, about a half inch from one side. The first hole on each side should be three-fourths of an inch from the end of the tube and the second hole on each side should be about one-fourth of an inch further on. A reference to the illustration will make this clear.

A rubber band is cut — thus giving a single strand rather than a loop. A knot is tied in one end. The other end is threaded through the first hole on one side, out through the opposite hole on the other side, and then run back through the two remaining holes. The free end of the elastic is knotted to prevent the rubber slipping through the last hole. Thus we have two strands of rubber running across the tube near one end.

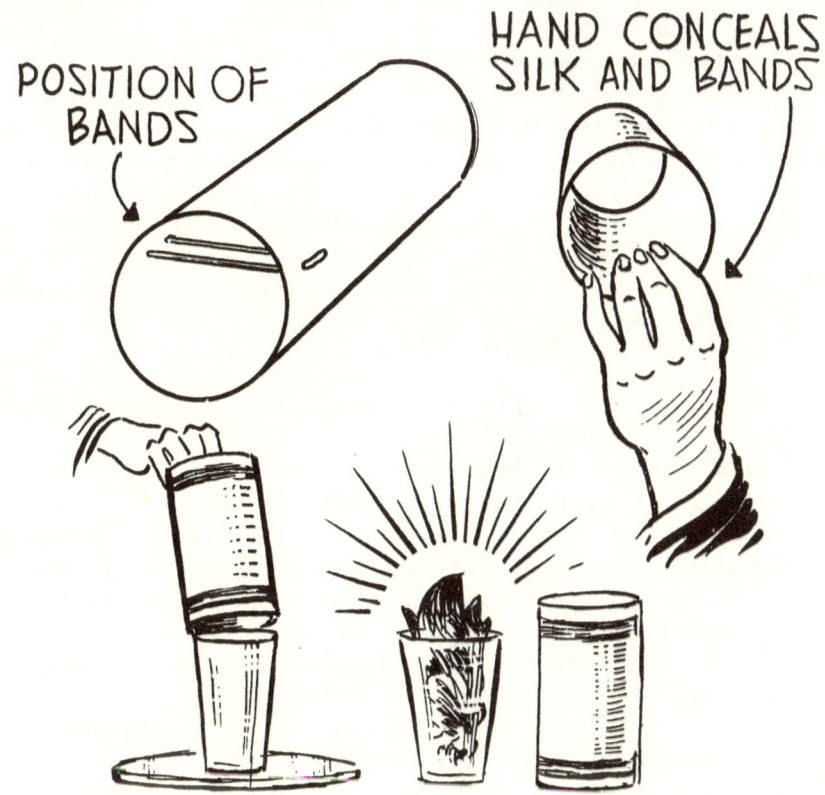

POSITION OF BANDS

HAND CONCEALS SILK AND BANDS

Considering the simplest effect first, the production of a single silk in the glass. It will be necessary to roll up a silk and tuck it under the rubber strands. There it will be held securely, but may be quickly dislodged by merely pushing it down with the fingers. In showing the tube empty—rather, apparently empty—the tube is held with the fingers on the inside covering the silk which is secured therein. This effectively conceals the silk from the all too inquisitive eyes of the audience. The tube, prepared end up, is then placed over the glass. The fingers of the hand holding the tube dislodge the handkerchief. It drops into the glass and unfurls, the tube is removed and magic has been done.

In accomplishing the color change, the tube is prepared in the same way. Let us presume that a red silk has been put beneath the rubbers. The tube is placed over a glass in the same way as before and the red silk is dislodged so that it falls into the glass. Now the magician shows another silk—green. This green silk is rolled up and seemingly dropped into the tube. Actually, however, the green silk is pushed beneath the rubbers, where it is destined to remain. Raise the tube, concealing the green silk with the fingers, and show the red silk in the glass.

The twentieth century effect is accomplished in similar fashion. Three silks, red, yellow and green, are knotted together, bunched up and deposited beneath the rubbers. The tube is placed over a glass and the three silks are dislodged. Duplicate red and green silks are knotted together, rolled up and placed under the rubbers. A duplicate yellow silk is vanished, the tube is raised and the trick is over.

Chinese Money Trick

By Silent Mora

I believe this to be one of the most surprising tricks with money that a magician can do when the audience is close up. The moves produce one series of astonishing effects after another until the climax is reached. Laughter and surprise are provoked among those who have not seen it before. Even if you have seen it you will enjoy the looks of astonishment on the faces of the rest of the crowd.

You will need three coins. The top coin in the illustration is hard to get. It is a Chinese coin about one hundred years old. The middle coin is 17th century Japanese, I believe. There are lots to be had. The lower coin is 6th Dynasty Chinese and almost impossible to find. Real ones are expensive, but there are some good imitations, which sell for about six dollars. If you are a mechanic, you can make your own money from brass and cut in the background with acid. An engraver can do this for you. If you have the patience to "get up" this trick, you will have something few magicians have ever seen. It takes a great amount of skill, but is well worth all the time you can devote to it. You can buy two of the coins from a collector of rare money, but you may have to make the other coin which, because of its shape, is called "man-money."

The basis of this effect is the vanish of a coin in the fold of your trousers. I invented the move accidentally many years ago when I was with Nate Leipzig. He vanished a coin from a trouser fold using an elastic. I worked out a reverse fold to the one he used. Leipzig said: "Mora, that's another new one." It has since been described in many books without credit to me.

In this one, you pull up the leg of the left trouser a little bit and fold the material down. This is done with both hands. Now place the coin in the fold with the right hand. The audience sees the coin against the pants, but they do not see the fingers of the right hand continue to slide the coin under the fold to the last two fingers resting on the trouser. Press the fold flat with the thumb and fingers of both hands and, in this action, the right hand has a chance to palm the coin. Once the coin is palmed, straighten out the fold, open it up, and the coin has vanished. With a little practice you can do this easily.

Now for the complete sequence. Produce the round coin from someone's lapel. Vanish it from the pants fold. Produce it where you will. Apparently bend the coin between your hands. Give it to a spectator, ask him to try and bend it. As all eyes are on him, steal the oval coin from your pocket with your left hand. Take the round coin back, bend it again. Say: "Never catch it by the extreme end, for you are liable to get it out of shape." Bring your hands together. The round coin is at your right fingertips, the oval coin is concealed in your

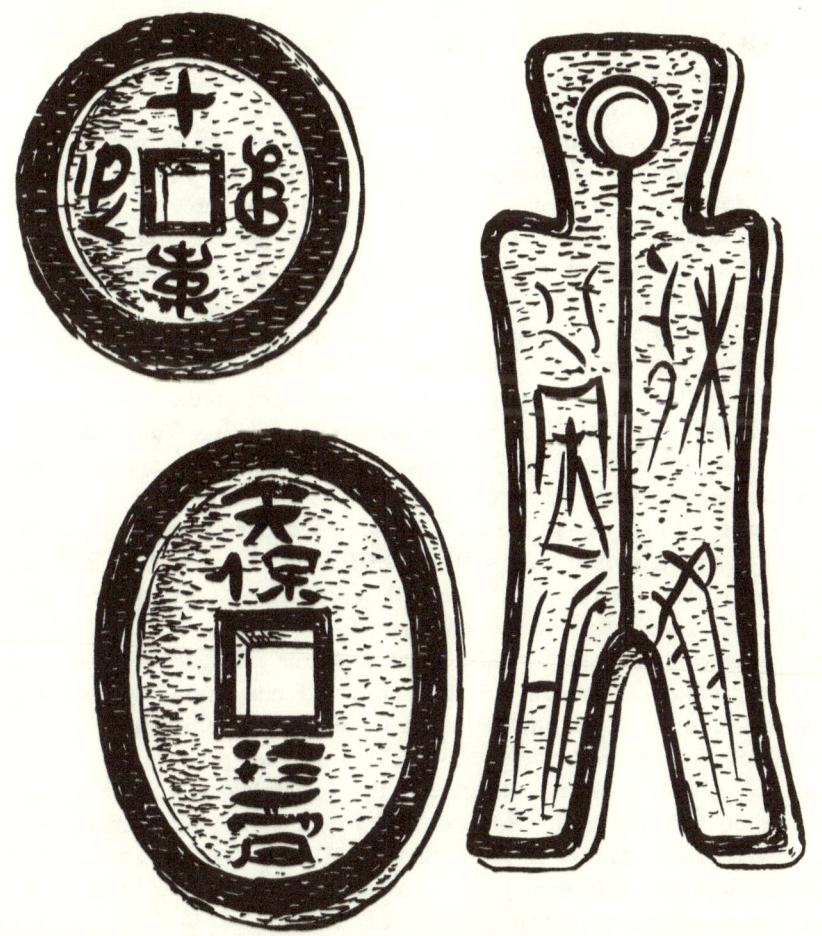

left hand. Conceal the round coin in your right hand and bring the oval coin into view. Pass it out to be inspected. Meanwhile get rid of the round coin in your right coat pocket and pick up the long coin. Turn your body away for an instant to hide this action. Take back the oval coin. Your left hand holds the long coin secretly by the middle fingers at the top joints and the base of the thumb. Say "Now, the most difficult part of this trick is to get it back in shape. You pull on the sides but not too much or you will get it completely out of shape." Bring the man-money into view, still pulling on it. They will howl when they see this one.

Your Card, Sir?

By Jean Hugard

This is an elaboration of a somewhat old experiment with playing cards. The requirements are: a small table, a pack of cards, and a small sheet of plain glass about six by four inches.

Begin by inviting a spectator to assist, and ask him to bring his hat with him. Seat the gentleman on your left, show the hat and place it crown down on the table, taking the opportunity now to press the sweatband open a little on one side. Have the spectator take the pack, shuffle it to his own satisfaction, and retain one card, handing the rest of the pack back.

The next step of having the card returned to the pack, brought to the top of the deck and, if desired, palmed off while the rest of the pack is shuffled I leave to each individual's pet method, suggesting that one that is as good as any is the Hindu shuffle. Take the pack now, replacing the palmed card on top and have the spectator cut the deck in two parts as nearly equal as he can manage it. Let him touch one. If he touches the packet with the chosen card on top, say: "I am to use this one, very well." On the other hand, if he chooses the lower packet, say, "You wish to have that one. Very good, take it please." Continue, "Now I want you to do exactly as I do." With that, take your packet and rip it in half. Place one packet down and rip the remaining packet in half again. Place these two quarter packets face down on the table, and pick up the other half packet. Tear this in half, and place the resulting quarter packets beside the others. While you are doing this, the spectator will probably be struggling with his half. However, take no notice. Go right on.

Pick up the quarter packet which looks to you to be the smallest, as they will probably vary in size. With the back of your hand to the audience, dribble out these pieces in a stream into the hat. At the same time pull back the top piece of card into finger palm position. Take up the next largest quarter pack and repeat the operation. Continue with the other two, keeping the largest until the last, since this will aid in holding the other three pieces easily and cleanly. Dip the last of the pieces into the hat and stir them around, taking this opportunity to slip the four palmed pieces under the sweatband, which you have previously pulled out a little to make this operation easier.

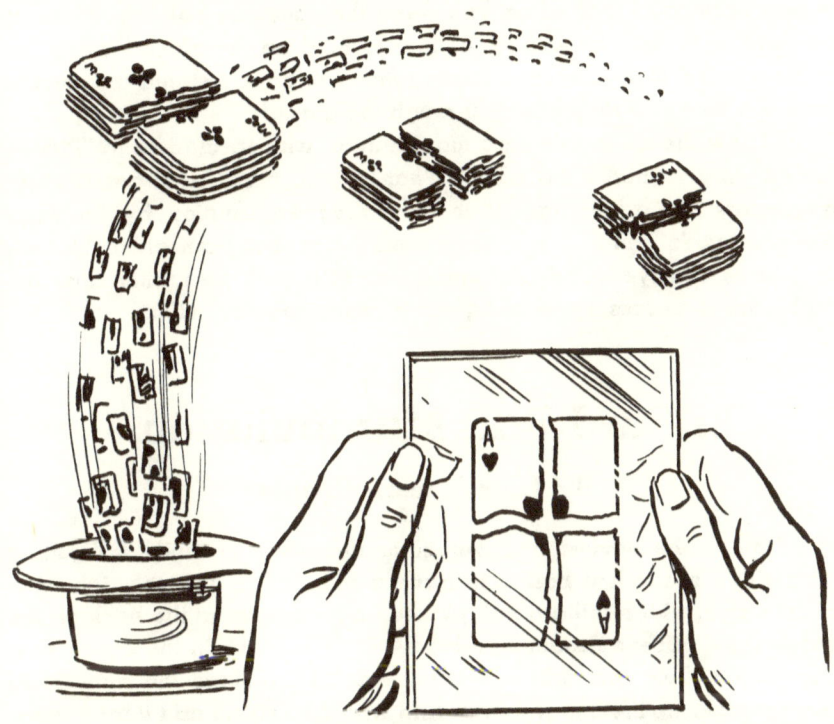

Now grasp the hat with the fingers inside covering the position of the four pieces, with the thumb outside on the brim, and turn your attention to your assistant. Probably he has not succeeded in tearing his packet in half even, but in any case let him finish the operation of quartering his cards over the hat, so that the audience sees the pieces drop in with the others. At this time it is advisable to recapitulate to the audience what has been done—a card has been chosen, the pack shuffled and the whole pack torn into quarters.

Now introduce a sheet of glass, on one side of which you have previously placed four tiny pellets of wax so that they form the corners of a square in the center of the glass about one and one-half inches apart. Hand it to the spectator and have him hold it in full view. Touch his hand with your fingertips under the excuse of getting the vibrations of the chosen card. Show your hand perfectly empty and carelessly dip it into the hat and draw one of the pieces of the chosen card from under the band. Hold it with its back to the audience and press it face down on one of the pellets of wax on the glass. This operation you repeat three times, but for the last one, let the spectator himself stir the pieces in the hat thoroughly, then touch his hand again and bring out the last piece.

The pieces, of course, have been placed in proper position on the pellets of wax so that when you have the spectator call the name of his card, it is only necessary for him to hold up the glass toward the audience and everyone sees at once that you have restored the chosen card, the face showing plainly through the glass.

I know the up-to-date card manipulator, who specializes in "Please take a card. Shuffle the pack. That is your card," will possiby not appreciate the advantage of the so-called explanation by touching the spectator's hand. I can only assure him that I am old-fashioned, and have always found that some sort of a plot, no matter how improbable, is necessary to bring out a really magical effect.

Billiard Ball Manipulation

By Herr Jansen (Dante)

One of the easiest and yet quite deceptive methods for getting possession of the first ball is to have a high silk hat at the right side of the stage, with a billiard ball placed under the rim at the back on the order of the Miser's Dream coin load, Figure 1. Now in the act of moving the hat from the right to the left side of the stage the right hand merely picks up the hat at the rim and with the second and third fingers, the ball is rolled into the palm. A net can also be stretched across the inside of the hat, and a wand laid across the opening. This will answer as a servante later on. The same hat, without the servante arrangement can be used for coin catching, etc. This is merely so that it is used for a purpose other than the real one.

I am indebted to Mr. Henry Clive for another method that I have used to great advantage. This consists of a billiard ball fastened to the middle of a china plate. The plate is arranged on its edge, bottom side toward the audience, with the ball side against the back of the chair, which stands to the performer's left. Now pretend to catch the ball with the right hand, then apparently put it in the left bulging out the fingers as though it were really there. The right hand picks up the plate, and as the ball side is gradually turned toward the audience, the left hand approaches it and quickly opens as though actually placing the ball there, Figure 2. The ball should be fastened to the plate

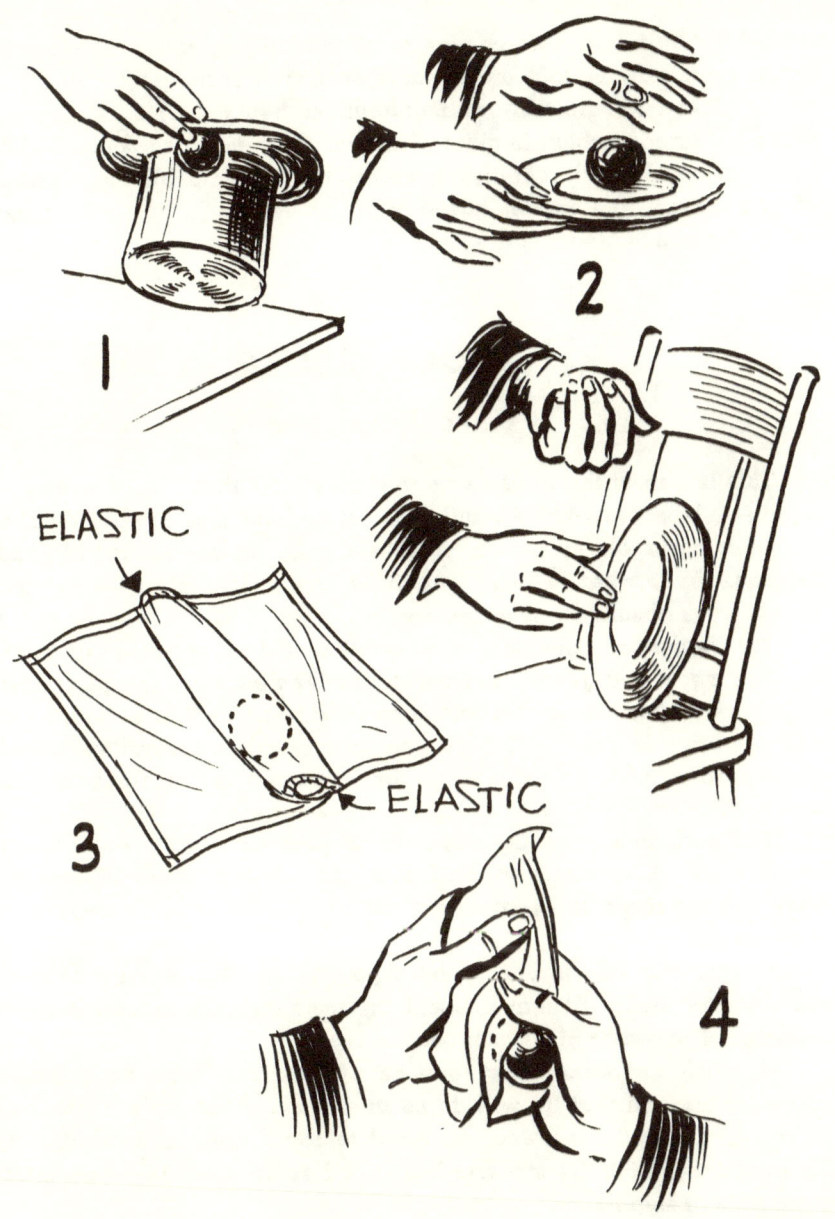

ELASTIC

ELASTIC

in such a way that it has a slight movement and rolls around a bit when the plate is shaken. This makes the effect perfect.

An ordinary handkerchief can also be used to advantage by doubling it over in the middle, then sewing it together so as to form a tube large enough to admit one ball.

Fasten a piece of elastic in the bottom of the hem tight enough to hold the ball, but loose enough to permit easy release. This hand-kerchief can now be laid on the table or placed in the pocket and yet can be picked up carelessly without anything being noticed. Performer wipes his hands, which is quite a natural thing to do previous to billiard ball work, and secretly squeezes the ball into his right palm. Several passes are made, however, to prove the hands are empty before the ball is produced.

Number Please

By Theo Annemann

This is one of the most extraordinary effects that I have ever put together. It is probably the only feat of its kind that doesn't require a code or signal of any nature. Your assistant can be coached in three minutes. And, what is more important to me, the effect — not the method — is absolutely new and original.

The performer asks that a committee of two or three take the medium away and guard her carefully until called for. The performer then asks a spectator for his telephone number, which is written on a strip of paper as given. The first spectator selects a second spectator, the second a third, and this is continued until a list of numbers has been written and verified.

The performer tears the paper in sections and drops each piece into a cup. A spectator mixes the pieces. The medium is brought back into the room and seated at a distance to the audience with her back to all.

A spectator selects one of the slips and takes it to a far side of the room to read. At that moment the medium calls out the correct number. The owner of the number verifies it.

Now the performer states that he will continue with the remaining numbers and that he will do so in silence. Each time a number is correctly stated the owner is asked to stand and acknowledge it. This continues until the medium has called every number. And there is no code or signals.

Method extraordinary: The first man or woman asked for a number unknowingly acts as a plant, because it is the host or hostess, whose number the performer knows. This is The Yogi Force, which Charles Jordan put out in 1922. From here on each spectator picks another which will make further working on this principle impossible.

Before starting the performer had two pieces of opaque paper about 2 by 5 inches. On one, spaced evenly, is written the known number eight times. The second piece is then placed on top of the writing and the two pieces are perforated together with an unthreaded sewing machine or a dressmaker's tracing wheel. Thus you have a "single" sheet of paper, which can be shown freely on both sides and is so perforated as to be torn in eight strips. After the first — the known number is written, seven other numbers are added as they are called out.

Tear the strips apart, holding the paper so that the writing faces you. Fold in half as you would to crease, then open each strip back out and tear off. Actually only one thickness of paper is opened out and torn off. This is placed on the audience side of the paper. Again fold the paper in half and this time open out only two thicknesses, tear off and place in front. Repeat once more and open out four thicknesses, and you apparently have a packet of single strips in your hand. Actually you have eight separate pieces, all alike, in the front and behind them the eight original numbers folded up and still together. Holding the packet in the left hand, the eight separate pieces are counted into the cup, the folded section is retained and the cup is given to a spectator to hold above his head and mix the papers. At this time the medium is brought in, and the performer takes her by the hand a second to help her to the chair. A good point here is to have the committee blindfold her, then it is perfectly natural to assist her as she goes to the chair. She gets the folded paper from the performer's left hand.

There are now eight papers—all like—in the cup. When the spectator takes any one, the medium, with her hands in her lap, opens the folded strip and calls the first name. It has to be correct. It is!

The performer takes any one of the seven strips remaining. The medium merely calls one of the remaining numbers on her list and the owner of the number verifies it. This procedure is continued until all the number are named. The fact that the medium calls the number and the man in the audience verifies it takes all thought from what the performer has in hand. What the audience will try to do will be to catch signals or discover how the magician is tipping off the medium.

Modern audiences are far from dumb, but they're out of luck with this test because instead of the performer telling the medium, she's telling him.

A Hat Load

By Birch

After the magician has produced a few dozen handkerchiefs, a paper coil or a few big foulards, it is easy enough to get extra loads in the hat under cover of the first production. The difficulty has always seemed to me to be to make the first load satisfactorily.

The following method I have used for a long time, and it is so natural that the audience has no idea that a' load was made. At the beginning of the trick I pick up a closed opera hat with my right hand. In my left hand I hold by my thumb a load of spring flowers. The number of flowers to be used must be found by experimentation. You will want enough flowers, when opened, to make a heaping hatful. I snap the hat open with my right hand, and hold it up so that it may be seen to be empty. I then transfer it to my left hand, catching hold of the hat with my thumb on the outside of the brim, and my fingers and the load inside the hat. Then attention is called to the bottom of the hat, which I tap with the fingers of my right hand. While holding the hat up in the air, crown down, I let go of the flowers. My assistant walks on the stage with a basket. I take it and pour the flowers into it. I manage to spill one or two on the floor. I notice the error and look down while my assistant picks them up and drops them in the basket. Just as I look down and my assistant stoops, my right hand brings the bottom of the basket over the hat for a fraction of a second and my first real load is made.

The basket is specially prepared. It is seven inches high and seven inches in diameter at the top. The sides taper so that the bottom is five and a half inches in diameter. The real bottom, however, is three inches from where the bottom would naturally be. My load is held under this false bottom by three clips, two of them stationary, the other movable. The movable clip has an arm which extends four or five inches up the side of the basket and is held in place by a spring. A slight pressure on this arm and the load is released from the basket. I use a five-inch paper coil as the bottom of the load and have silks, or whatever else I plan to produce, packed on the coil. Of course it is possible, but I have never found it necessary, to have a removable reed bottom for the basket. It is easier to remember to keep the bottom away from the audience.

If a magician does not use an assistant, he could momentarily set the basket on top of the hat, while he stooped to pick up the flowers himself.

In order to have the basket attract no attention it must not be decorated in any way, but rather be the kind of a basket one would take out in the garden to fill with flowers. I had my basket woven specially with the false bottom made right into the basket. This is not expensive and is well worth while.

Comedy Cigarette

By Lu Brent

Here's one for the comedy performer. Extract a banana from a paper bag. Peel it and eat it with much gusto. Now, after every good meal a good smoke should follow, so — take a cigarette from your pack. Peel off the paper as you did the skin from the banana. Light it and smoke with great satisfaction.

The cigarette peeling is very funny since the tobacco does not fall apart. Why? Because you have one of those little cigarette-shaped cigars with a piece of white paper glued around it. It looks exactly like a cigarette. Perform this in pantomime.

The Ramo Samee Card Trick

By Dai Vernon

Before mentioning this trick, it should be noted that in the excellent volume, "Magician's Tricks and How They Are Done," by the late Henry Hatton and Adrian Plate, is a feat they describe as "one of the most incomprehensible tricks ever invented." While the Hatton and Plate trick is excellent, it depends upon the use of a deck of but 32 cards, and that I do not care for. Further, it depends upon the performer's memorizing several tables. As my method uses the entire deck and does away with tables, it is actually new. The feat is a favorite with several of my magician friends and I call it by the name they have given it — "The Ramo Samee Card Trick." Ramo Samee, an East Indian magician, was the first recorded performer of his nationality to appear in America. There is nothing East Indian about the trick — but then you know how it is with a name for a trick.

I deal four poker hands. Quite naturally, I deal myself the best hand, but this is all merely preliminary to the trick. Once the hands are seen, I "happen to recall" another feat. I ask someone to think of any card in the deck. The choice is entirely mental and he neither touches a card nor writes down the name of the one he has in mind. Then quite naturally, I pick up one of the hands of poker just dealt, and ask if there is a card of the same value among those in the hand. The second hand is shown in the same way, and the same question is asked. The third and fourth hands also are shown one at a time, and the same query is made. On these last two hands the further question is made as to whether, in these hands, are cards of the same suit. Immediately after these questions, the magician announces the name of the card held in mind by the spectator.

The secret consists of the choice of the cards in each of the four hands. In the illustration are shown the cards I suggest that you use. Variations in the choice of the cards may be made, but you will find the cards suggested work well with audiences. In the illustration alongside the hands are the numbers 1-2-4-8.

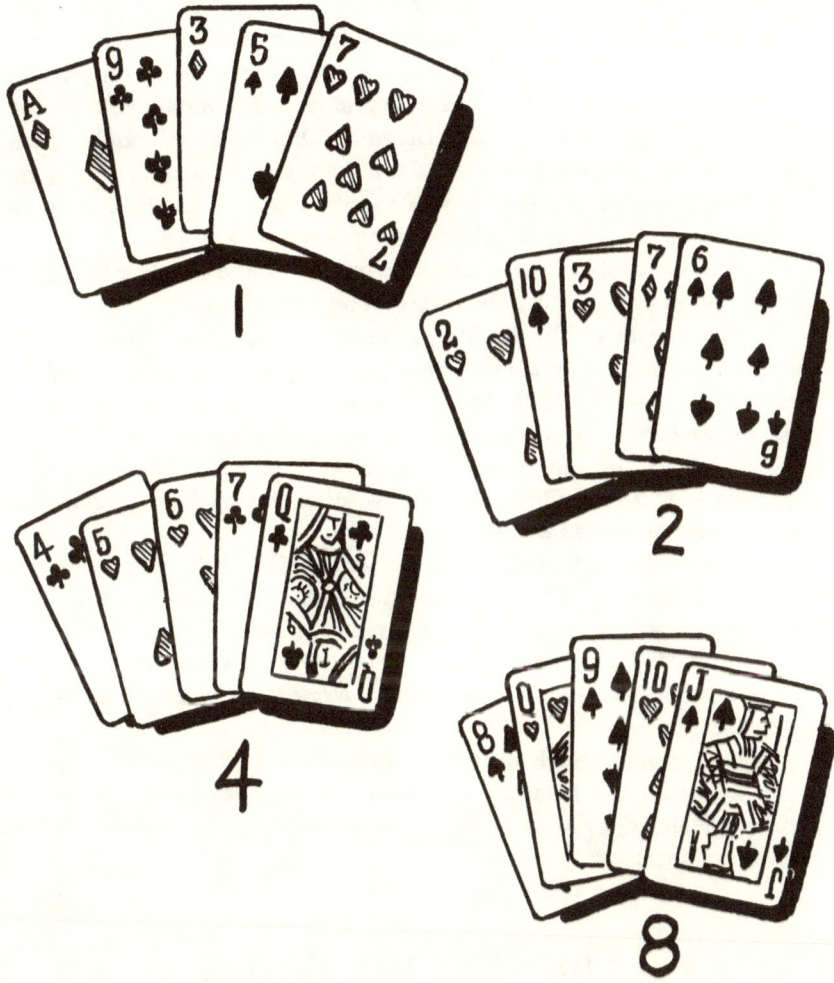

First please consider the method of discovering only the value of the card. This is done by adding together the numbers of the hands. As an example, if the mentally selected card appears only in the first hand, the total number is 1 plus 0 plus 0 plus 0, or 1. One is the same as Ace—therefore the card is an Ace. If found only in the second hand, the card is a Two. However, if it appears in both the second and third hands, but only those hands, it is a Six, because the numbers of those hands—2 and 4—when totalled make 6. There are but two exceptions to this rule. If a card of the value thought of is not seen in any of the four hands, the card held in mind is a King. If the card value is found only in the last hand, the card thought of is either an 8 or a Jack. This Jack is the only card for which any fishing need be done. The magician can say "Is it a picture card?" If it is a picture it must be a Jack, and if not a picture it must be an Eight.

Now as to suit. If the two hands shown in the bottom row of the illustration are studied, it will be seen that clubs are found only in the hand numbered four. Hearts will be found in both hands, while spades will be seen only in the hand numbered 8. Diamonds will not be found in either hand. Therefore, when the magician asks if a card having the suit of the one held in mind is seen in either or both of the hands, he will know by the answer which suit it is.

If found in both— hearts, and if in neither— diamonds. If only in one hand— clubs, and if only in the other— spades.

In order to have the hands made up of the cards illustrated, of course the deck must be set up either prior to performance, or, for those having the necessary skill, during the performance of other tricks. It is not necessary to set up the pack so that poker hands may be dealt. I like that idea, but others may wish merely to count off four sets of five cards—"merely indifferent cards"— after the pack has been shuffled. Of course a false shuffle is indicated.

It is very simple to remember the value of each hand, for the first hand is numbered 1. The second is twice one, which makes it 2. The third is twice two, or 4. The last is twice four, or 8.

The description on paper may make the trick sound involved, but it will be found very easy to perform. Work it on yourself, using the illustration.

This is a trick which may be repeated several times without the secret becoming the least bit apparent. After a few trials, it will be found possible, easy and most effective to "read the minds" of two persons simultaneously.

The Napkin Ashes

By Joe Rukus

Tear a paper napkin to bits, set it afire and let it burn to ashes on a plate. Take the plate and pour the ashes on the palm of your outstretched left hand. Place a bottomless glass, mouth side downwards over the ashes, as in Figure 1.

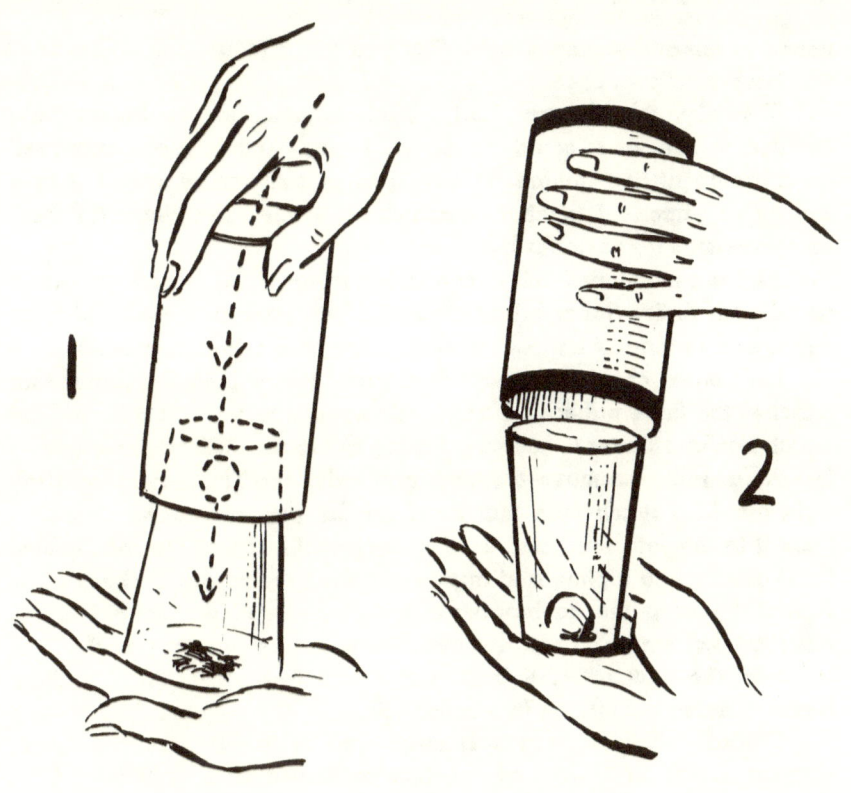

Now secretly palm a duplicate, balled-up napkin, which has been hidden behind a metal tube on your table, in your right palm. Pick up the tube with the right fingertips at the top and put it over the inverted glass in your left hand. Release the palmed napkin which falls through the bottomless glass into your palm as you cover the glass. Place your right hand over the upper end of the cylinder and turn the works upside down.

Lift off the tube. There in the glass is the restored napkin. Tilt it out in your left hand, put down the glass and hold it out between your hands for display.

Laurant Cashes His Own Check

By Eugene Laurant

Whenever I am called upon to present a stunt at a banquet, I usually tell a story about how I was once obliged to cash my own check. "Most of us," I say, "have experienced difficulty in attempting to cash a check in a city in which we are a stranger. This once happened to me and someone said, 'But you are a magician. Why don't you cash your own check?'

"Frankly, this thought had never occurred to me before so I decided to see what could be done. I made out a check to myself for the sum of five dollars. I tore it in pieces and wrapped it in a square of paper. I touched a match to it, the wrapping vanished, and there was a five-dollar bill."

As I tell the story I suit action to the words. The trick is prepared as follows: A five-dollar bill is crumpled, wrapped in a piece of flash paper and put in my left coat pocket, along with a box of matches.

I fill out a check to myself and wrap it in a piece of paper that matches the flash paper. I hand it to someone to hold. I take out the match box and under it, secretly, I bring along the flash-paper-wrapped five-dollar bill. I remove a match and strike it. This I hold with my right hand. I reach with that hand for the paper-wrapped check. I pass it to my left hand and hold it against the top of the match box. I call attention to a plate and apparently drop the wrapped check on it. Actually I drop the flash-paper-wrapped five spot. I get rid of the other packet when I drop the match box in my left coat pocket. A touch of the match to the flash paper and it vanishes in a brilliant flame, leaving behind the five-dollar bill.

I think this idea was first suggested to me by my old friend Stewart Judah of Cincinnati. I first presented it at a Rotary Club luncheon. After that I frequently used it as a publicity stunt.

The Hanson Kewpie Doll Illusion

By Herman Hanson

A large, lettered toy block is seen on the stage with a large toy balloon floating above it. It is tied to the box with a half-inch-wide silk ribbon. The ribbon runs through the top of the block and is fastened to the inside bottom with a small thumb tack. The front doors of the block are opened, and the cabinet is wheeled around to show it unmistakably empty.

A small kewpie doll is placed inside the cabinet, with one hand outstretched as if it is holding the ribbon. The doors are closed. The cabinet is again wheeled half a turn to show that nothing is concealed in the back. The block is seen to grow, or slide, upwards, as a second block comes into view. When the cabinet is double its original height it splits apart revealing a live girl, dressed as a kewpie doll, who still holds the end of the ribbon.

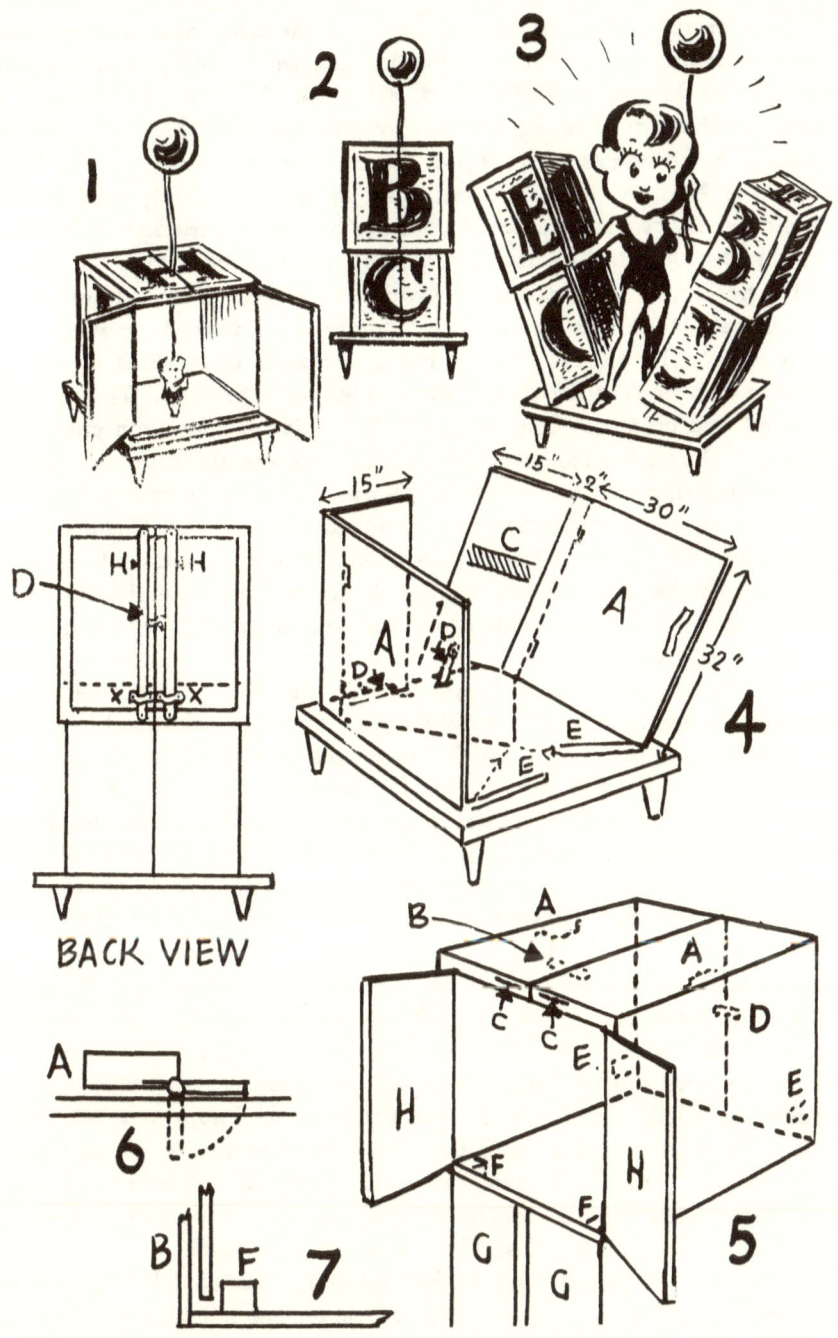

BACK VIEW

Modus operandi: An assistant, who wears a papier mache kewpie head and is dressed to match the doll, is concealed behind mirrors, Figure 4, A-A. The ribbon holding the balloon conceals the front edge of the mirrors. When the front doors are closed, the assistant immediately closes the mirrors flat against the side walls, and places the doll in back of the white elastic band, Figure 4, C. After the cabinet is turned to the rear, then back to the front, the assistant places her head exactly in the center of the top of the cabinet and takes the handles, Figure 5, A-A, one in each hand, and, at the cue, slowly pushes the outside shell, or block, upward until the hinges, Figure 5, E-E, are automatically closed. The assistant then opens the hook, Figure 5, D, and, at the performer's cue, pushes the two halves apart to reveal herself.

Construction: The inside block is made of solid wood, three-quarter inch stock. The outside block is made of frames of two-inch by three-quarter inch stock with canvas glued on the sides and top. The canvas is sized and painted. The inside block should be lined with cretonne. Figure 4 shows the inside of this block. A-A are the mirrors. These are hinged and pull to a forty-five degree angle to conceal the assistant. B-B are the handles that hold the mirrors in position. C is the wide elastic band for holding the kewpie doll. D-D are large desk fasteners, which hold the blocks when split. E-E are half-inch metal bars, one-eighth of an inch thick, which hold the two cloths G-G at the bottom edge. I-I are hinges.

In the outside block, Figure 5, A-A, are the flat handles, kept against the top with small spring hinges. B is a metal dowel fastened to one half of the block, which must work freely in the hole of the other half block. C-C are buttons for locking the doors H-H. D is a flat hook on the inside, which keeps the two halves of the block together. D is also shown in the back view. E-E are spring hinges, with weak springs, made to close instead of open. Being between the inside and outside blocks, when the outside block is raised they open over the edge of the inside block, Figure 6, A. Figure 5, F-F, are the wooden blocks, which keep the outside shell on the inside block at the front, Figure 7, B. G-G are cloths tacked to the bottom of the frame of the outside shell and are fastened to the metal bars E-E of the inside block, forming the missing side of the inside block. In setting the illusion, the cloths are folded between the bottom frame and E-E. The cloth should be of the same material, which lines the inside block. H-H, shown in the back view, are metal bars one-eighth inch by one-half inch fastened on the inside of the shell. They slide in X-X sleeves, preventing the falling of the halves of the outside block.

Remarks: I would suggest that the stage curtains be opened to show a child's playroom, with the block on the left and, perhaps, a large ball or hoop on the right. A girl assistant, in kiddie costume, is playing with the kewpie doll in the center.

For patter, the magician could find out from the child that, although she has plenty of toys, she is lonesome for a companion. The magician says that if she will let him use her doll and the block, he will create a playmate for her. This he does to the delight of the little girl and the audience as well. Of course, any other doll could be used instead of a kewpie doll.

Penetration Deluxe

By Keith Clark

Put a lit cigarette in your mouth. Hold an 18-inch silk at one corner with the left hand, one corner of the silk lying at the inside of the bend of the arm, as in Figure 1. Turn your right side to the audience. Take the cigarette in the right hand, between the index and middle fingers — smoker's position; bring it over the center of the silk, and apparently wrap the silk around it.

What actually happens is this: When the cigarette is over the silk, the right third finger rests on the silk-covered palm, Figure 2. The left hand turns over and drapes the silk over the right hand holding the cigarette, which is immediately transferred to the thumb grip, screened by the folds of the silk, Figure 10. The right thumb is extended upwards at once, taking the place of the cigarette under the silk, Figure 4. The right fingers are curled around the cigarette to protect the silk. All this takes place during the one continuous gesture of wrapping the cigarette in the silk.

Figure 3 shows the position of the hands and the cigarette just as the silk is about to be tossed over the right hand and the cigarette thumb palmed. Figure 4 shows the position after all of these actions have been completed.

While you still stand with your right shoulder nearest to the audience, the left hand approaches the right hand and the left fingers close around the cigarette (really the right thumb) through the silk, seemingly to grasp it and carry it away, Figure 5. Withdraw the right thumb as the silk is being removed, so that it isn't disclosed sticking up in the air. Drop the right hand for an instant to call attention to the left hand, and impress on the audience that the cigarette is now wrapped in the silk.

The right hand, back to the audience, now goes behind the left hand holding the silk and, under cover of the left hand, transfers the cigarette to a position between the right index finger and middle fingers — smoker's position. Now, it is promptly transferred to a vertical position between the left thumb and index finger, lighted end up, where it is clipped with the silk. The lighted end must be above the silk so it cannot come into contact with it, Figure 7. The right hand closes

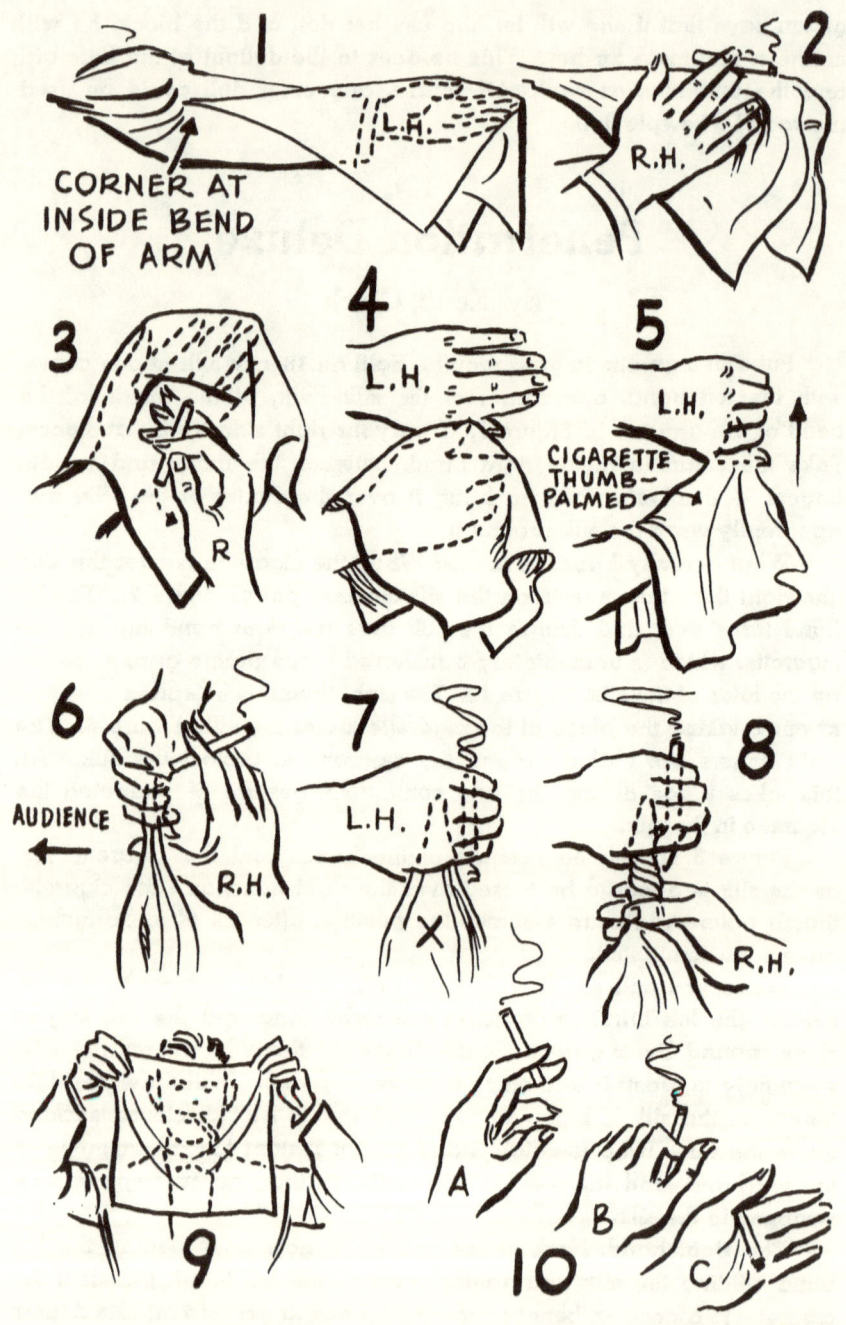

around the silk below X, Figure 7, and twists it several times. As it twists, the left thumb pushes the burning cigarette out of the left hand, as in Figure 8, and it seems to have burned its way through the silk.

Study Figures 2 and 8 carefully and practice these moves until perfect. Practice with an unlighted cigarette first.

Take the cigarette with the right hand and place it well between the lips. Show the silk to be unharmed by holding it up between the hands, as shown in Figure 9, and bow to the applause.

Martin's Twelve Card Trick

By Tommy Martin

In offering this version of the classical card effect known as "The Cards Up the Sleeve," or "The Twelve Card Trick," it should be stated that although an effect of this nature has been performed for years by various conjurers, in one form or another, it has, for the most part, been accomplished by a certain set series of manipulations, which in the following treatise have been virtually eliminated. In eliminating these sleights, I have substituted in their place a new series of simple and easily mastered moves, which have been universally accepted as the most effective and baffling method of presenting this greatest of all card effects. As will be seen in the following explanation, the performance of the effect will depend, for the most part, upon the showmanship of the performer. Due to the fact that a number of cards, held in full view of the spectators, are caused to vanish one at a time until each in succession is reproduced from the performer's trouser pocket, there is a tendency toward the presentation becoming monotonous unless the performer introduces a certain amount of personality and showmanship in order to entertain the spectators throughout the feat. The following explanation makes an entirely new effect of this time-honored bit of card conjuring.

Presentation: The performer holds a number of cards in his left hand, which are counted and proven to be exactly twelve. He asks the indulgence of the audience while he proceeds to cause these cards to disappear one or two at a time until each card in succession has mystically vanished from the hand. The cards are reproduced from the right trouser pocket. At all times the cards are in full view of the spectators, and, properly presented, their evanishment is as bewitching an effect as there is to be found in the realm of conjuring. Their subsequent reproduction from the trouser pocket heightens the mystery of the effect considerably, as the cards may be noted and memorized by the spectators if the performer chooses. Several new moves together with a number of invaluable and sure-fire methods of misdirection serve to render this presentation easy to master and, at the same time, positively baffling at all points of the procedure.

Secrets: Previously, put two cards in the upper vest pocket; one card, a spade, is placed in the watch pocket of the trousers and three cards are "top-pocketed" in the right trouser pocket. (By "top-pocketing" is meant the placing of cards in the upper part of the pocket, so that the lower part may be pulled out and shown as empty.) In the right trouser pocket is, also, a coin, which serves later on in the effect.

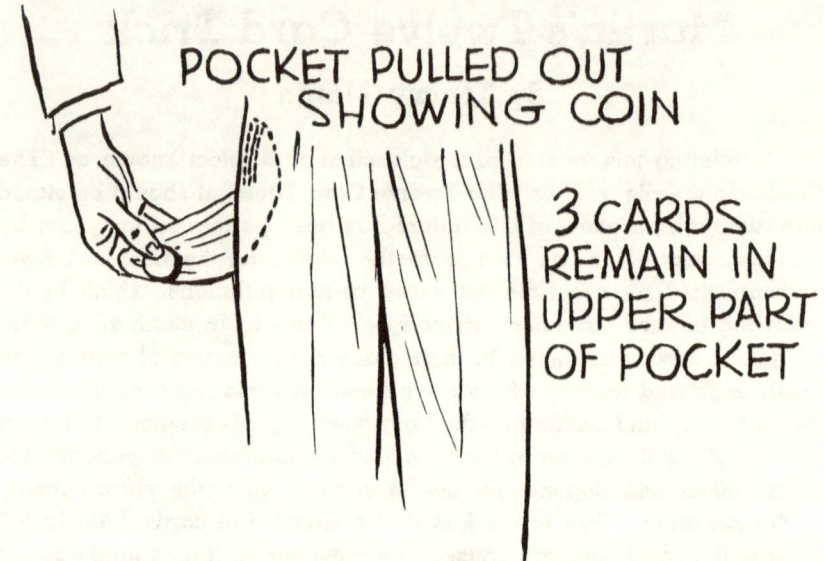

POCKET PULLED OUT SHOWING COIN

3 CARDS REMAIN IN UPPER PART OF POCKET

Opening Remarks: Advancing toward the spectators with only nine cards in the left hand, the performer begins:

"Ladies and gentlemen, I should like to offer for your approval an effect with a number of playing cards. I shall hold the cards you see here at arm's length and each time that I say 'Go,' or each time that I tap the cards, while you are watching them they shall disappear one at a time in the air or, better still, I shall have them make their way across the vest and down into the trouser pocket, which as you may observe contains nothing but this half dollar, which has nothing to do with the performance, nevertheless I shall leave it here." (While saying the above, the performer pulls out the right trouser pocket partially and shows the coin; the three cards remain hidden from view in the upper part of the pocket.)

The performer continues: "I should like you to watch the cards closely, and see if you can see them go. Watch. So that all may understand the procedure, one, two, three, etc.—on up to twelve cards are used." (Begin counting the nine cards to appear as twelve, holding the backs of the cards towards the audience. Bring the two hands together and, in removing one card, call out at the same time "One," and, in continuing, go through this same motion, but on the count of cards number two, four and six fail to remove a card from the hand, which will cause the nine cards to appear as twelve, since three of them have been counted twice.) This false count is explained and illustrated in several well-known treatises on card conjuring. After having counted the cards, begin passing them in the following fashion:

In beginning the actual effect, riffle the nine cards twice, creating by this move two crepitating sounds and saying simultaneously "One" and "Two." Show the right hand empty, then say, "Cards, numbers one and two have begun their journey, and we find them in this right trouser pocket. (At this point, two of the top-pocketed cards are brought out one at a time, shown and placed on a table.)

"You may doubt that I am passing these cards, but I had twelve and have passed two, so that leaves (now count the nine cards, using a false count on one card so that they appear as ten) ten."

Hold the nine cards in the left hand and ask a spectator to hold your left wrist, saying: "Will you hold the wrist, please, and I shall pass one card through your hand and mine." Again riffling the cards, ask: "Did you feel the card go?" Count, as you say: "It must have gone, for we have only nine cards left." With the faces of the cards toward the spectators, show them to be nine in number. Advancing toward another spectator, have him remove the third, and last, of the top-pocketed cards.

Remark, "You did not take the coin, did you?" Reach in the pocket to verify this and introduce six cards, which were palmed from the nine in the left hand as the spectator removed the card from your pocket. In introducing these cards top-pocket them, and pull out the pocket, showing the coin is still there. Leave the pocket out, put the coin in another pocket.

"Watch closely." This time rap the remaining cards in the left hand with the right hand, saying: "As we watch them, two more cards begin their journey and are found in the—" (Performer, seeing the pocket hanging out, remarks: "Oh, the pocket is out; I shall push it in and catch those two cards before they get back to the left hand.") The two cards, previously placed in the upper left vest pocket are withdrawn as the left side is turned toward the audience.

Showing the backs of these cards, the performer, with his left side still toward the audience, reinserts them into the vest pocket and taps the sleeve on the outer side of the coat, remarking: "Perhaps this is silly, but if you remember the cards, you shall see that they will arrive, for here they are." Two of the six cards previously introduced into the top of the pocket are shown and placed aside.

Again rap the cards smartly and say: "Two more shall begin their journey." Show the right hand empty and remove two more of the cards from the trouser pocket.

"As the pack grows smaller, less pressure is required to make them go." Suit actions to words, and say: "Another card is on its way." The right hand reaches into the watch pocket, as the performer says: "It must be a spade, for it is digging me." The card is withdrawn with the remark, "This one did not quite arrive." Now say: "We have passed eight cards and, just as a matter of checking up, eight from twelve would leave how many?" As the answer—four—is given, false count the three cards to appear as four. Hold these cards at the finger-tips, the arm well extended, the right side to the audience.

"I shall tap these four, and we have left only three." (The three cards are counted. The right side remains towards the audience.) Place the three cards back in the left hand, show there is nothing in the right hand and remove another of the top-pocketed cards from your trouser pocket, which is away from the audience. (This must be timed so that the audience, in watching the card emerge from the trouser pocket, does not see the performer slip one of the three in the left hand into the left coat pocket.)

Turn towards the audience, hold the last two cards together, tap them and say, "Go." The two cards are now shown and slapped together with an inward and outward motion from the face to the length of the arms, enabling the performer to wet one of the cards, as it touches his face. Place the two cards together and say: "I shall now pass one more . . . Go." Toss the two remaining cards a foot or so into the air. (The cards adhere because one was moistened and pressed against the other.) They appear as one card. Show the front card, adroitly palm the hindermost card, at the same time pass the front card from the right to left hand. Let us see if it has arrived." The palmed card is now introduced into the pocket, and removed as if it had been there for quite some time.

For the evanishment of the last card, a number of suitable sleights for the disappearance of one card are to be found in books dealing with card sleights, but one of the most effective vanishes is to simply palm the card in the right hand. In the act of shoving it into the left hand, the left hand remains closed as though it held the card, while the right hand, which really contains it is moved rapidly towards the pocket. The right thumb and fingers roll the card so that it is held in the crotch of the thumb. The fingers thus appear apart. When the left hand opens, the right hand inserts this last card, straightens it out in the pocket and withdraws it. "So thus the last card reaches its destination."

If one is fully adept in the basic moves of card magic, the preceding effect can be easily mastered. If not, seek personal instruction from some performer familiar with these moves, as it is often very difficult to learn them properly from reading a description of how they are accomplished. Hoffmann's "Modern Magic," and "The Expert at the Card Table," by Erdnase, carry graphic illustrations and detailed descriptions of the basic moves. The misdirection with the coin at the irntoduction of the cards is both subtle and novel.

An Alcohol Rub

By Howard Savage

A calling card is handed to the sitter, who writes a question on it. The medium opens a small envelope, address side down, for the reception of the face down card. The envelope is immediately sealed.

When the medium places an identification mark on it, he not only tells the sitter his question, but also answers it.

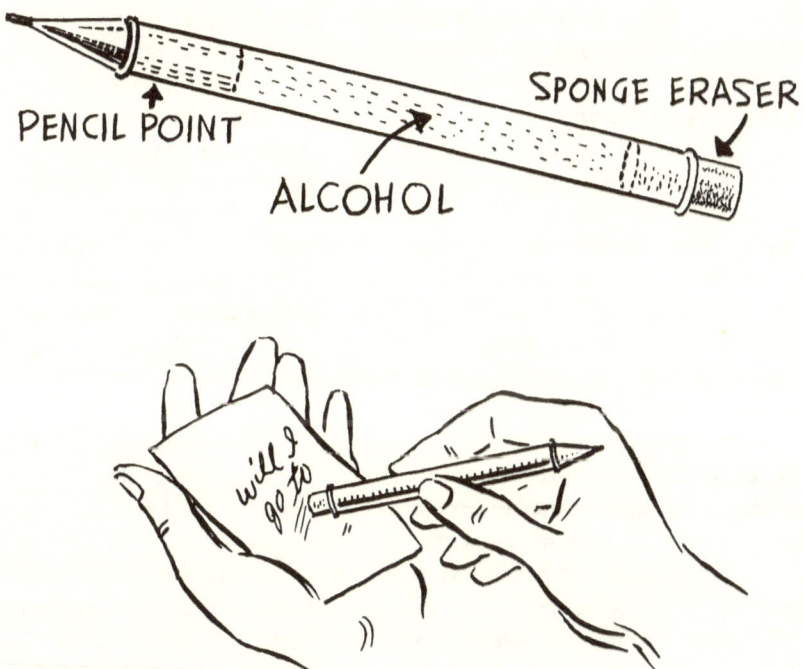

The mystery's solution lies in the solution, alcohol, that is in the hollow metal pencil of the medium. He pretends to make a mistake and erase it, but really moistens the envelope with the sponge-rubber false eraser, thereby rendering it transparent.

The chemical dries rapidly and the question is handed back after a lengthy answer.

Jack Trepel's Telephone Book Trick

By Jack Trepel

This is a method whereby a spectator is allowed to open a telephone directory at any place he chooses, other spectators signify a choice of name on that page, and the magician is able to know both the person chosen as well as the telephone number.

In the presentation the magician gives a telephone directory and a pencil to a spectator. The magician then picks up a slate and a piece of chalk and sits on a chair with his back toward the audience. First, he instructs the spectator to open the book at any place he chooses. He then asks for someone else to call out "left-right" or "right-left." For example, right-left is named first. The magician asks the person holding the directory to look at the right hand page and call out the number so that anyone who wishes may check on each detail later. The magician then announces that as right was called first, that leaves left and that the person holding the directory should put his pencil at the top of the left hand column of the chosen page. The magician asks another person to call out a number. He suggests, in order to keep the experiment from becoming too lengthy, that the number should be from one to twenty-five. The spectator holding the directory is asked to count down the column until he comes to the name designated by that number. For example, if twelve is called, the spectator would count to the twelfth name. He is then asked to mark the name with a pencil, to read it to himself and, in order to impress it on his mind, to draw a circle around it. Next he is asked to read the telephone number to himself and likewise to circle it.

The magician rises, faces the audience and reminds the spectator who is holding the directory that he had a free choice of any page and therefore, as a matter of fact, a choice of any one of the thousands of names and telephone numbers.

The magician writes a name and number on his slate and holds it, reversed, over his head, by the fingertips of one hand. The spectator holding the directory is asked to stand and read loudly, for all to hear, the name and phone number he has chosen. Before he is finished, the performer turns his slate toward the audience so that it may be verified that he has successfully predicted the correct name and number.

Method: Prior to the performance the magician cuts a segment from the bound side of the directory four inches long and a little over the width of one column. This gives the magician a small bound book, having the beginning of the right hand column of all the left hand pages, and the beginning of the left hand column of all the right hand pages. In a majority of the directories issued by the telephone companies, if not all of them, the pages are numbered at the center of the book. It will now be obvious that provided the spectator announces the number of the chosen page, the magician will be able to turn to that page. The spectator, seemingly, is given a choice by naming right-left or left-right, but it makes no difference which is chosen. In either instance there will be indicated the part of the page that the magician has in his miniature directory. Limiting the choice to a number under twenty-five again keeps the choice within the section held by the magician. In the directories with which I am familiar, a four inch segment of the book gives twenty-five names. It is advisable to check the number of names in the directory you will use and limit the choice of numbers accordingly.

ELASTIC

The magician's small directory is attached to a length of elastic which goes around his body through either the belt loops of his trousers or the loops of his suspenders. The end of the elastic is looped around the binding of the book between the pages. At the beginning of the trick, the book is pushed inside the top of the trousers. After the directory has been given to a spectator, the magician picks up the slate with his left hand, the chalk with his right. A slate is more impressive, though a pad and pencil may be used. He turns his back to the audience by swinging to his left. In making this turn his left hand goes out so that the audience may see the slate, while his right hand goes in front of his body and removes the small directory. The magician then sits on the chair and puts the slate on his lap. Inside the directory is a small flat pencil. As soon as the magician locates the name and number in the directory, he writes both on the wooden frame of the slate. He then releases the directory and the elastic pulls it inside his coat as he stands. I use this pull because I found that any unusual movement on my part such as putting the directory in my pocket attracted unfavorable attention. There is plenty of time to locate the page while the spectator is deciding on the number between one and twenty-five, and also ample time to write down the name and number while the spectator is counting and encircling.

The magician then stands and impressively calls attention to the impossibility of guessing one name from so large a choice. He writes both the chosen name and number on the slate, disclosing to the audience that he has read their minds.

The reader is warned to be sure and watch his angles and to have no spectators seated on the sides of the room, where they may be in a position to see the method used for the trick.

Levante Flowers from Cone

By Les Levante

A girl assistant, who wears a short frock with an apron of flowered pattern, hands a cornucopia made of newspaper to the magician. He shows that it is empty. He shakes it a bit and suddenly it is filled with flowers. The assistant holds the ends of her apron between her hands to catch therein the flowers that pour from the cone. The flowers continue to materialize until an unbelievable total of 300 is produced. The magician tears up the cone; the assistant carries the flowers off stage. The effect is self contained. The magician has nothing to pick up, no tables, no fuss. When the trick is over, the stage is clear.

Needed: Three bundles of spring flowers, each held by a dual elastic band. The details of the elastic holders are clearly shown in the illustration. When the release pin is pulled, the flowers expand. A cornucopia made from a double sheet of newspaper. It is about 18 inches high. One bundle of flowers is put in the bottom of this cone. It is covered with a small piece of newspaper, which is tucked around the flowers so that the cone can be shown directly to the audience as an empty cone. In fact, I hold the cone right up to a spectator, practically pushing it in his face. The release string at-

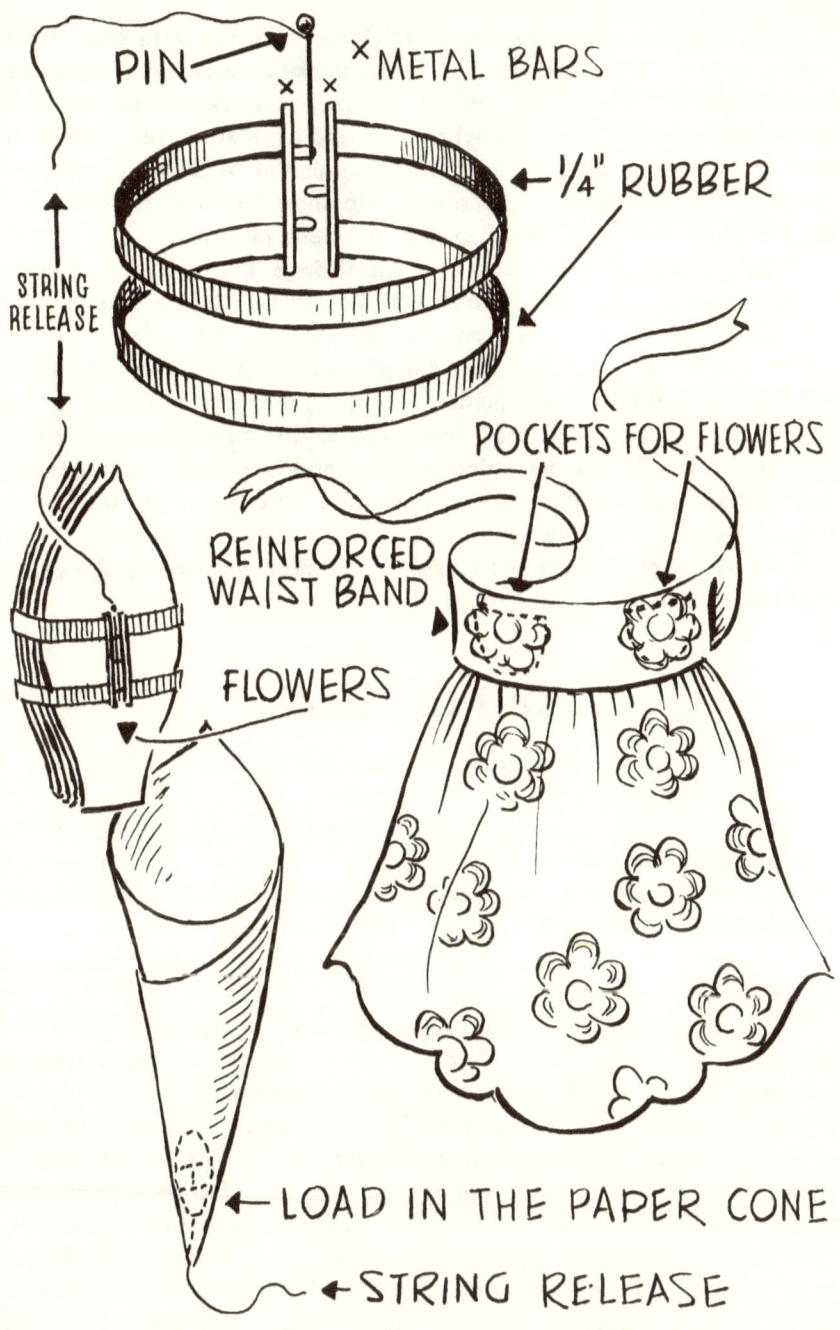

PIN
×METAL BARS
¼" RUBBER
STRING RELEASE
POCKETS FOR FLOWERS
REINFORCED WAIST BAND
FLOWERS
LOAD IN THE PAPER CONE
STRING RELEASE

tached to the pin is threaded from the inside through the bottom of the cone so that it hangs outside. On the reverse side of the girl's flower patterned apron up near the belt, which ties around her waist, is sewn an eight inch wide strip of buckram. On the front side of the apron, over the buckram, are two secret pockets made from the same material as that used in the apron. Each pocket is attached so that the material blends perfectly with the overall pattern. The bottom of each pocket is sewn in place right through the buckram. The tops of the pockets are held in place with two snap fasteners for each. A bundle of flowers is enclosed in each of these pockets.

The routine begins when the girl brings the newspaper cone to the magician. He shows it empty, then at the right moment pulls the release string. The flowers expand and fill the cone. The assistant holds out her apron and the performer sprays it with flowers. With his free hand the magician, in helping the flowers to fall in the apron, is able to pull a load from one of the pockets and throw it into the cone. When the string on this load is pulled, more flowers are released and a further stream flows into the apron. The third load is obtained in the same way.

When the production is completed, the magician rips up the cone, and the girl exits.

Find the Lady

By P. C. Sorcar

The card trick, "Stung and Stung Again" or "Fooled Again," is known throughout the world to the magical fraternity. I have improved the feat and present it with extra large size cards. This makes it a phenomenal success on big stages. The cards, 12 inches by 18 inches, are made of three-ply wood. They are hand painted on both sides and polished.

On the stage stands a nickel-plated stand, on which hangs a flat canvas bag, slightly larger than the cards. There is a Sphinx head painted on the bag with the name Sorcar under it.

As I enter, I bring three cards held in a fan. They are the Jack of Clubs, Queen of Hearts and the King of Clubs. I slip them inside the bag in full view of the audience, and ask the audience to remember the names of the cards. Next I say: "The Queen of Hearts is not here. She is gone. As proof I pull out the first card, the King of Clubs. I hold the bag upside down and slide out the Jack of Clubs. Where is the Queen? I hear someone say that it is still in the bag. I at once pull the zip fastener in the bottom of the bag, which reveals a big card on which is printed "Fooled." Every Tom, Dick and Harry calls to see the opposite side. I am, at first, reluctant. Finally I turn the card, only to show the words "Fooled Again."

Secret: The bag is specially constructed. The design on the front is upside down on the back. This is so that the bag will look correct even when inverted. A perfect illusion is created because the act of reversing the bag shows the second design, right side up. Any other way of turning the bag would be too obvious. There is a small section in the bag where I conceal the "Fooled" card. It cannot fall out when the bag is reversed and can only be extracted when the zipper is unfastened.

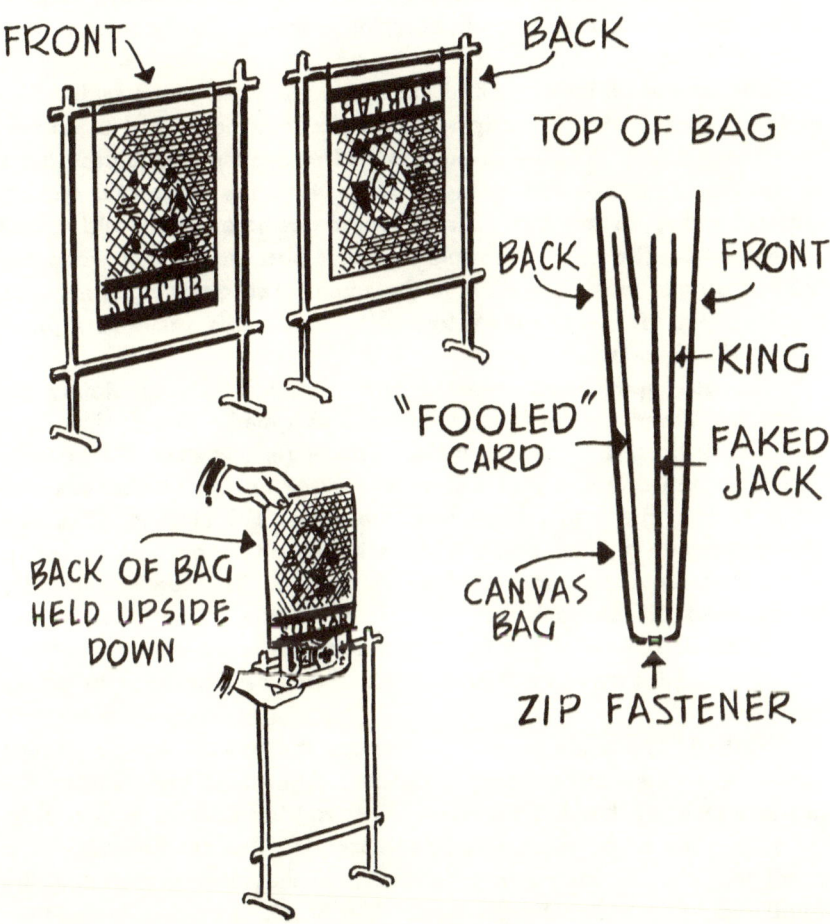

The King of Clubs is unfaked. The second card is prepared. The Queen of Hearts and the Jack of Clubs are painted side by side, as if they were held fan-wise, on the face of this card. A normal Jack of Clubs is painted on the reverse side.

Keep the "Fooled" Card in the bag from the beginning. Show the other two cards, fan-wise, so they look like three cards. Put them in the bag and follow the outlined presentation.

The Weigh of All Flesh

By Al Baker

The orchestra plays soft, slow music as the curtain goes up. The professor is standing on the stage at the side of a blackboard which is on an easel. In the center of the stage, hanging on a rope from the flies is a dialed scale with a large hook. The hook is about six feet above the stage. The magician claps his hands, the music increases in tempo, and two coolies come in carrying a trunk. The magician says nothing, but acts interested.

The coolies lift the trunk and hang it on the hook of the scale. The scale registers just 75 pounds. The magician turns toward the blackboard and writes "Trunk—75 pounds." The coolies then lift the trunk off the hook, unstrap and open it. They leave the stage and quickly return, leading a slave girl. The magician gestures that the girl should be weighed. The girl is wearing a leather harness, so that when she is lifted up she may be hooked to the scale. The girl weighs an even hundred pounds, so the magician writes under his previous figures: "Girl—100 pounds."

The girl, upon being released from the hook, is immediately put in the trunk and the trunk is locked and strapped. The coolies once more hook the trunk on the scale. The scale registers 175 pounds. The magician draws a line under the figures on the blackboard and totals them. His sum agrees with the scale, 175 pounds. The magician picks up a pistol, points it at the trunk and shoots. At the sound of the shot, the scale jumps back to 75 pounds. The coolies hurriedly lift the trunk off the hook and put it on the stage. They unstrap and unlock it. They open it and tip it toward the audience so that everyone can see that the girl has disappeared. Everything is done in pantomime.

Method: The scale is faked. Perhaps the easiest way to do this would be to take an ordinary accurate, large scale and remove the rod to which the hand is fastened. This rod is replaced with a tube, to which the scale mechanism is attached. Inside this tube is a small rod, a coil spring and a catch. Until the catch is released, the small rod is controlled by the tube. The hand, of course, is fastened to the small rod. Upon releasing the catch, the spring moves the small rod and the hand back the distance that the hand would have to travel on the scale to indicate 100 pounds. When the trunk is lifted down from the scale, the hand again goes to zero automatically, as the regular scale mechanism is not disturbed.

The method of causing the girl to disappear is by using the well known tip-over trunk — the trunk sometimes called the Crystal Trunk.

In this trunk, of course, the girl does not actually disappear but it seems so to the audience.

As a finale for the trick, here are two suggestions. One is that a twin of the slave girl comes running down the aisle of the theatre. The second suggestion is that one of the coolies takes off his coolie costume and it is the twin.

Naturally the figures you will use will be those of the weight of your trunk and your assistant.

Paper Balls to Hat

By Slydini

This is a pantomime routine to be performed while seated at a table. Four tissues are rolled into balls. They disappear, one at a time, from the hands of the performer and appear in a hat, which previously has been shown empty. The trick may be done close-up or as a platform feat before an audience of considerable size. The manipulation is quite simple, but the details must be memorized and carefully rehearsed to create the proper effect.

All that is needed is a hat, which may be borrowed, and four pieces of paper. I use facial tissues, these are sold under such names as Kleenex and Pond's Tissues.

The routine begins by the magician showing a hat, pointing out its emptiness and placing it, open side upwards, on the table to his left. The four tissues are shown and put to the right. The performer shows his hands to be empty. Then, with his right hand, he picks up a sheet of tissue and waves it several times over the hat. He turns left at the waist so that his right side — his head and trunk — is toward the audience. The hands are brought up to shoulder heighth and the tissue is rolled into a ball between his palms.

The magician closes his left hand around the ball, and points to his left fist with his right hand. He opens the left hand to show that the ball is still there. He picks it up with his right fingertips and raises the right hand high over the hat — the left hand drops naturally to the lap. He slowly lowers and raises the ball above the hat several times. This gets across the idea that the ball is to go in the hat, but the magician is very careful to have the audience see that the ball does not go into the hat. The ball is always visible.

The magician returns the ball to the position between his palms and rolls it once more as if to make the ball more firm. Figure 1. Then he moves his right hand away from his left, closing the left as if it held the ball, but really palming the ball in his right hand. The left fist is raised and the hand is turned over so that the thumb points downward and the palm of the hand is away from the audience. The right hand is lowered to rest gently on the edge of the table and the ball is dropped into the lap. The left hand is brought toward the hat and, as this move is made, the right hand is brought up to the left. Both hands are held some distance over the hat. The fingers of the right hand pry open the closed fingers of the left hand so that the audience can see that there is nothing in either hand. However, the magician acts as if he were still holding the ball and he drops the imaginary ball into the hat. He removes his hands from the vicinity of the hat and bends forward and looks in. He deliberately nods his head as though he were saying: "Yes, it is there."

The spectators can see that the magician's hands are empty, and understand that he claimed to have dropped an invisible ball into the hat. Actually the magician has the ball in his lap.

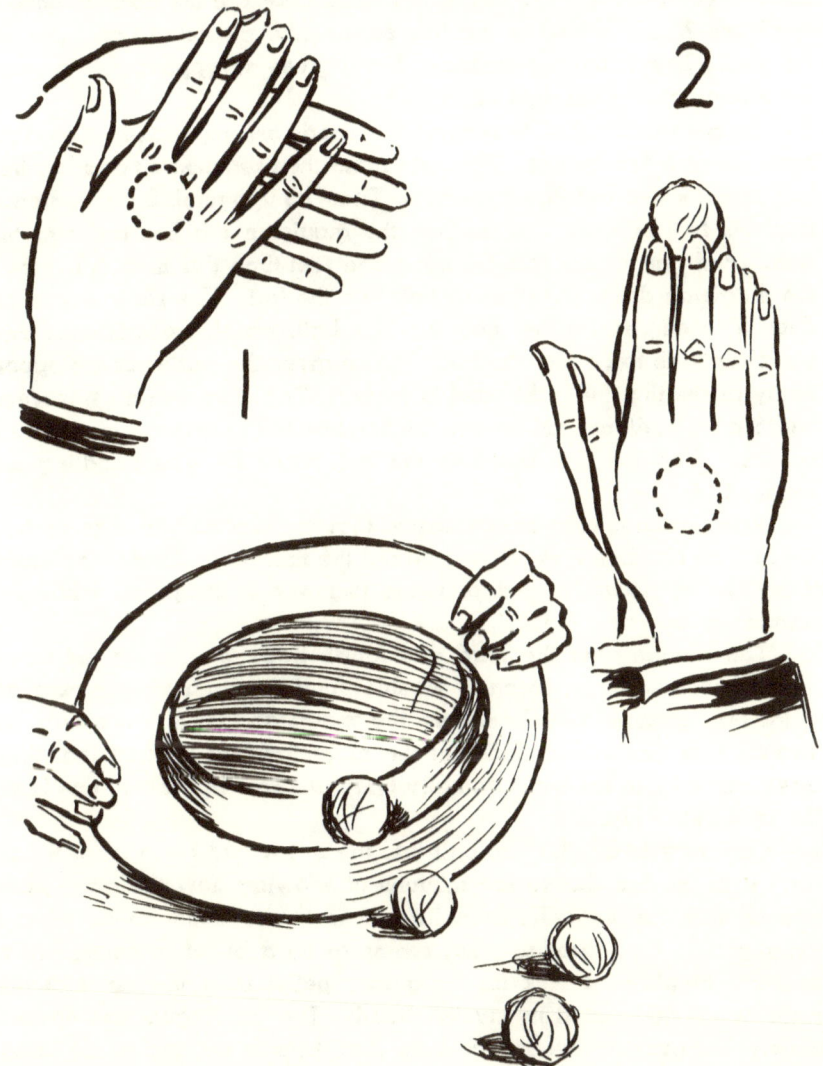

The magician now rolls the second tissue into a ball in the same manner he used in making the first ball. He exhibits it in the fingers of his left hand, while the right hand casually drops to the lap and picks up the first ball.

This ball is held in the palm by the thumb. Care must be taken to keep the back of the hand toward the audience so that the ball remains hidden. When the two hands come together, the visible ball is pushed up to the fingertips, Figure 2, and the hidden ball is squeezed between the palms of the two hands. When the hands are together, the hands, as if to better exhibit the visible ball, can be turned sidewise with the little fingers toward the audience. The palmed ball will be masked completely. The hands are turned back to the position shown in Figure 2, and raised to the lips so that the magician can blow on the ball. This is merely business, but it gives an opportunity to palm the hidden ball in the right hand.

As soon as the ball is palmed the hands are separated. The right hand drops a few inches. The right hand then reaches up and touches ball number two with the fingertips. Then, as if to remind the audience that this ball is to go into the hat, the magician reaches out with his right hand and dips it into the hat. The first time this motion is made the magician drops the palmed ball into the hat. The second time he does it to emphasize the idea that the ball, which the audience can see plainly, is to go into the hat. It also gives the audience an opportunity to see that the right hand is empty. The magician must remember that the audience did not see the first ball fall to his lap, nor did they see him drop the first ball into the hat, while he was handling the second ball.

After the magician has indicated that the second ball is to go into the hat, he handles it exactly as he did the first ball. That is, he drops it on his lap secretly, and pretends to make it disappear while his hands are held over the hat.

The routine with the third and fourth balls is actually the same as that used with the second. At this point the audience, to sum up what has gone before, has seen the magician cause three balls to vanish, and has understood that the magician has implied that they have passed into the hat. Actually three are now in the hat, one is on the magician's lap.

One way to get the last ball into the hat would be to palm it and drop it in the hat during the motions of showing how the other balls passed into the hat. However, it seems to me better to do what I usually do. I go through what seems to be a bit of inconsequential comedy by-play. I pick an imaginary pellet from the air with my right hand, and put it in my left hand. The left fingers are opened slowly, I show surprise and concern that there is nothing in the hand. I look higher in the air and grab with the left hand. Meanwhile, I drop my right hand to the lap, and palm the fourth ball. Then, in the same manner as I got the previous balls into the hat, I drop in number four. I open my left hand to show it is empty. I show my right hand empty. I pick up the hat carefully to show that there is no trickery, then I tilt the hat slowly toward the audience. The four balls spill out.

Switching Decks

By Harlan Tarbell

Modern-day magicians have often made something complicated that the old-timers accomplished in a simple action. One of these things is switching one deck for another. Various contraptions have

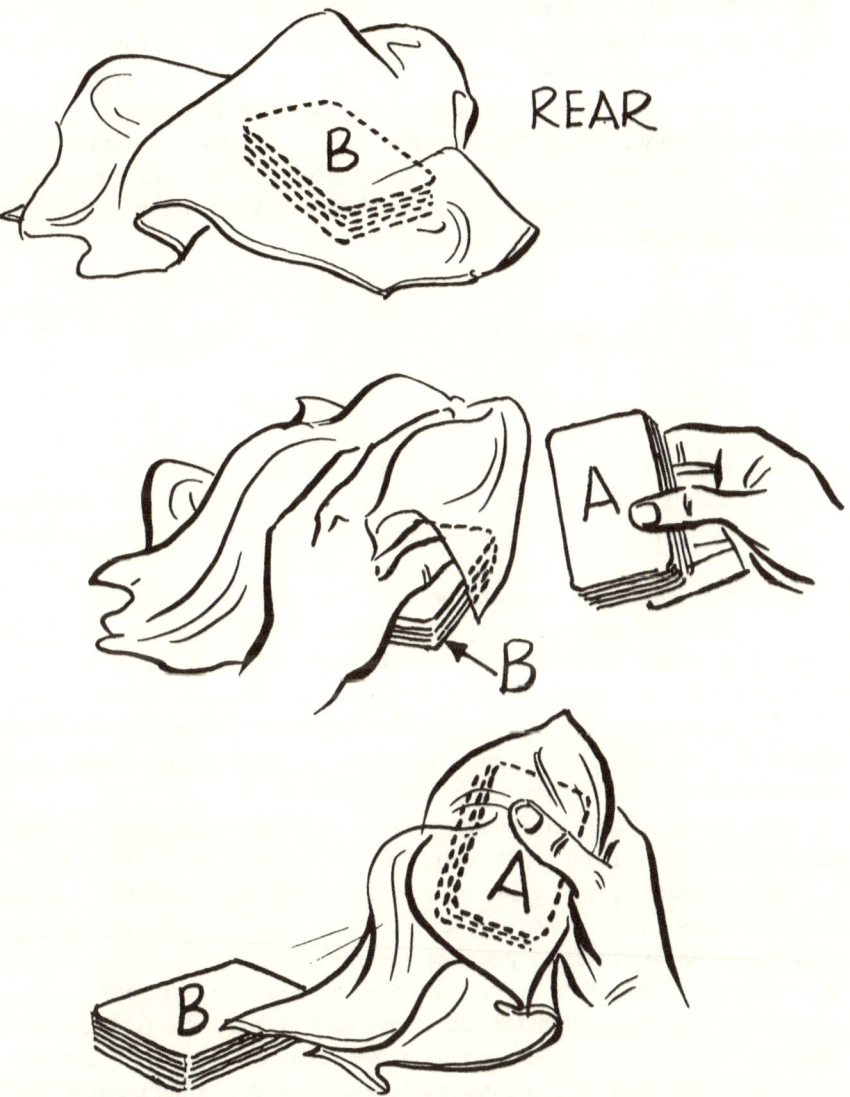

been brought out for this purpose, some of which seem far removed from the simple subject at hand. I am going to describe a method of changing decks, say a deck of forcing cards for a regular deck, or a deck of regular cards for a threaded pack, such as was used by Herrmann, Powell, DeKolta, Kellar, Ransom, Reno and many others. I, myself, have used it many times in performing the rising cards, where I wanted to switch a regular pack for one threaded for the card fountain.

The threaded deck B is on the table under a silk handkerchief, Figure 1. The audience, of course, is not aware of this hidden deck. Now, let's say that three cards have been selected, returned and shuffled in the pack. This deck is held in your right hand. Pick up the silk at the rear with the left hand, thumb underneath, and place deck A under it, Figure 2. Transfer the silk from the left to the right hand. Put the silk down on another part of the table in full view. All this is but a moment's work, and to the audience all that you have done is simply to place a deck of cards on the table and pick up a handkerchief, which is temporarily in the way, and place it aside. Try this method and see how easy and effective it is.

Flowers at Your Fingertips

By Milbourne Christopher

One by one the magician produces flowers at his fingertips and drops them on a waiting tray. When the tray is filled to overflowing, the magician reaches out again in thin air and produces a huge bouquet.

Method: This is a new and effective use for spring flowers. Previous to the performance a stack of 20 or 30 folded flowers is held under the tray by a clip. Another packet of 20, with strings attached to each, tied together in the usual bouquet fashion, is inserted in a second clip.

When you pick up the tray, your right hand steals the group of single flowers, the other hand cups around the bouquet stack, and masks it completely as your left hand holds the tray.

The closed fingers of your right hand hide the compressed flowers from view. To produce the flowers, press your right thumb against the top folded flower of the packet and push it forward. The flower props open instantly. It seems to appear from nowhere. Drop it on the tray and repeat the process to produce the other single flowers. As each is produced, it should be held a second or two, then dropped on the tray. See the illustration for the exact way to hold the flowers and produce them. E shows the stack in the hand as the thumb presses firmly on the top flower and shoves it forward. D shows the open flower at the moment of production at the fingertips.

Following the production of the last single flower, both hands hold the edge of the tray momentarily. The left hand grasps the bead on the

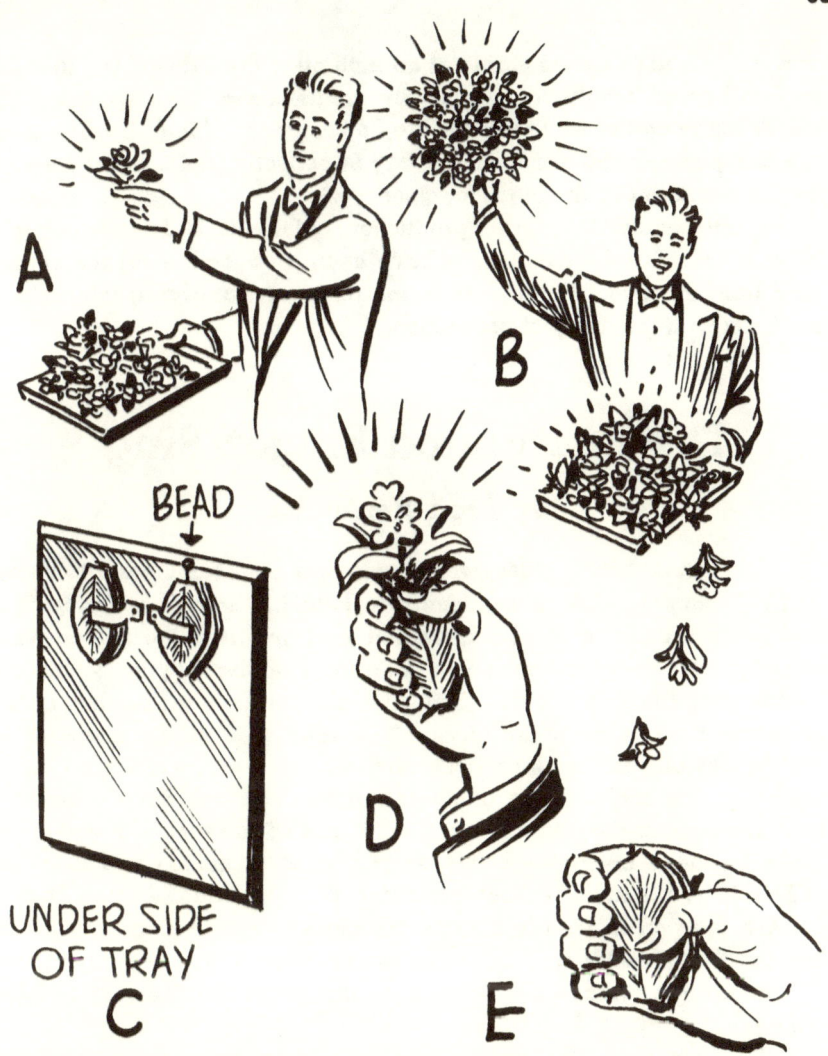

A

B

BEAD

UNDER SIDE
OF TRAY
C

D

E

knotted end of the folded bouquet and, holding the bead firmly, moves out and a dozen inches away with lightning speed.

The bouquet materializes instantly. The flowers cover the hand that produces it. This is your applause cue. Walk off with the bouquet in your left hand and the flower-filled tray in your right.

This can be presented under the most rigorous conditions. I have used it in the center of a night club floor. For full effect, use flowers of one color — red. They show up better and appear to be real flowers. Not so, the blue, yellow, green and purple assortments that are usually used.

Silk flowers, those with silk outer leaves, slide better than paper flowers. I had to cut an eighth of an inch off of the sides of my flowers so that I could manipulate them with greater ease.

A ledge on the tray prevents the flowers from falling off when they are dropped. In the diagram, the tray is perfectly plain, but a colorful design would mask the loads for close work.

Should you wish a larger production, enter with 20 flowers palmed in your right hand. After these have been produced, steal the single load from the tray. Finally, as in the other version, bring the trick to a climax with the bouquet production.

The Enchanted Finger Ring

By Leon Herrmann

Take an ordinary glass, which you pass for examination to show that it is empty. Ask a gentleman to hold it. Borrow a finger ring and place it under a silk handkerchief, and give it to the person who already holds the glass, as shown in Figure 1, so that at your command he can drop the ring into the glass, and also let the handkerchief go at the same time to cover the glass. Now take your magic wand, or a stick about one-half an inch thick and one foot long, which you have ready on the table. Take another handkerchief, which you borrow from someone in the audience, and roll it around the stick, but you must leave the ends of the stick free, so that another person will be able to hold it by the ends without interfering with the handkerchief, Figure 2. Ask the person who is holding the glass to shake it so as to hear that the ring is still there. Take the handkerchief that covers the glass by one corner, remove it quickly from the glass and the ring will be gone.

Now you go to the person who is holding the stick, and by removing the handkerchief, which is around it, you will find that the ring has passed onto the stick, Figure 3. The beauty of this very surprising trick is that the person who is holding the stick did not remove his hands from the two ends, still the ring will be seen on the center of the stick. It is one of the most beautiful sleight of hand tricks, entirely unknown, and has never been exposed. It is also one of the most effective to perform. It may be shown in a parlor with great advantage and, with a little practice, my readers will undoubtedly be successful in its execution.

Have a false ring attached with a piece of thread, about three inches long, to the center of a silk handkerchief. Have that handkerchief in the outside little pocket of your coat. When you borrow a ring from one of the ladies in your audience, take the handkerchief out of the pocket with your left hand (the false ring on your side), and with your right hand place the lady's ring, the real ring, in the handkerchief. As soon as the handkerchief covers the right hand, quickly exchange the real ring for the one which is attached to the handkerchief, and keep the real ring in the palm of the right hand while you hold the false ring through the handkerchief with your left. Give the covered ring to the person who is holding the glass and ask him to hold it over the glass so that, at your command, it will be easy for him to let it drop in the glass. Of course, everyone will hear the

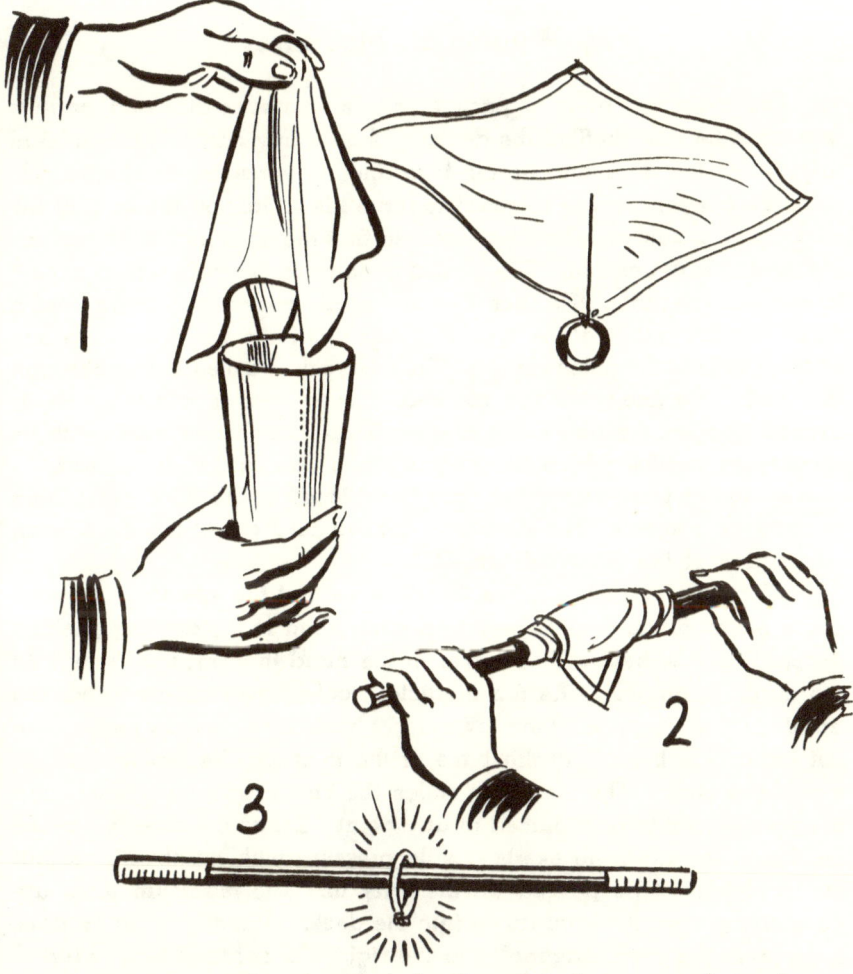

ring as it drops in the glass, as the thread is long enough to give a kind of loose balancing to the ring. Be careful that the handkerchief covers the glass all around, so that no one can see the ring inside.

Now take, by one end, the stick with the right hand, which has the real ring palmed, and manage to slip the ring over and on the stick, but always keep your hand closed to hide the ring. Now when you roll the handkerchief around the stick, twist the handkerchief around the ring and slip it to the center of the stick; it is only when you give the stick to someone to hold that you take your hands from the stick.

Cash and Change Purse

By William H. McCaffrey

The magician gives a pack of cards to a spectator and permits him, after he has shuffled the deck, to choose any card. The magician then takes the deck and hands it to another spectator to shuffle. He asks the one who chose the card to write his initials on the face of the card. The magician riffles the deck so that the spectator may replace his card in any position. The magician squares the deck and passes it to another spectator. He then reaches in his pocket and brings out a small change purse, of the type that has two nubs which overlap one another to hold the purse closed. The spectator is asked to look through the deck. He finds that the marked, chosen card is missing. He is invited to open the purse. Inside, he finds that chosen card, with its identifying marks, folded to one-fourth the size of the open card.

Up to the point where the card is replaced in the deck everything is quite as it seems. The sleight to get the card out of the deck is an adaptation of the "dove-tail pass."

When the magician riffles the deck so that the spectator may replace his card, the deck is held in the left hand in the dealing position except that it is held a little lower in the hand than most people hold the cards in dealing. As the magician looks down on his hand, the tip of his little finger is at the lower right hand corner of the pack. The left hand side lies along the base of the thumb. The top itself is on top of the pack. The magician riffles the cards, as I have said, and allows the card to be replaced at any point. Before the card is pushed too far in the deck, he exerts a little pressure with his thumb so that the card cannot be pushed all the way in. The magician then, apparently, pushes the card down into the deck. Actually what he does is to press the card diagonally to the right. In short, exactly what is done with the "dove-tail pass," but in the opposite direction. As the card is pressed around to the right, the fingers of the left hand straighten out. This, of course, is done under cover of the fingers of the right hand while the thumb of the left hand holds the pack together. The fingers of the left hand then curl back toward the deck and, if the moves are made correctly, the chosen card is held in the usual palming position in the left hand except that the cards of the rest of the pack are both above and below the chosen card. The left hand, as this "dove-tail pass" is made, is turned so that the back of it is toward the audience. The right hand takes hold of the pack, at the top, which is protruding out from the left hand, and pulls the pack away from the left hand, leaving the chosen card palmed.

As the pack is handed to the spectator, the left hand drops to the

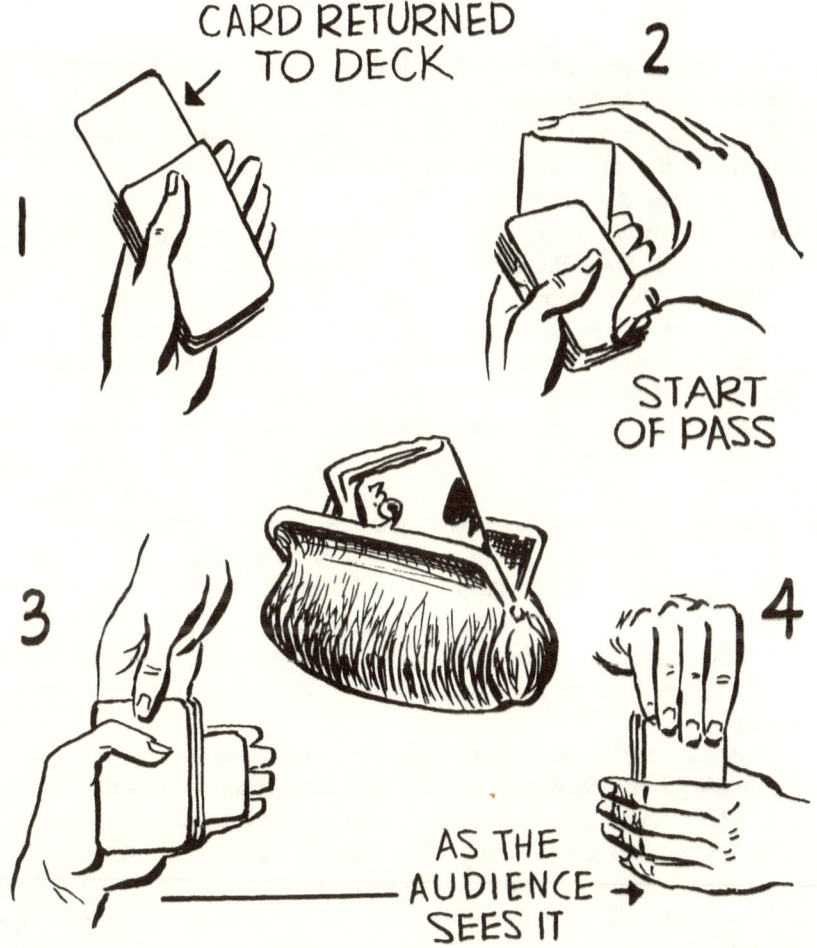

CARD RETURNED TO DECK

1   2

START OF PASS

3   4

AS THE AUDIENCE SEES IT

side. When you close the left hand, the card is folded in half. Then pressing with the thumb in the center of the folded card and permitting a little space between the second and third fingers, it will be found very easy to fold the card in quarters. The left hand then goes into the left coat pocket and pushes the unfolded card into the already open change purse. The purse is snapped shut and brought from the pocket and handed to the spectator. If this trick is done correctly, the audience not only will have no idea that the card could have left the pack, but will not dream that the chosen card could be found in the tiny change purse.

Rope-It

By Bob Haskell

A selected card is shuffled back into the pack by a spectator. The spectator spreads the cards in his hands and tosses them in the air. As the cards come down in a shower, the performer, who has formed a lariat out of a piece of rope, lassos the selected card.

Properties: A bobby pin, painted white, and a ten-foot length of rope. A lariat is made from the rope, and the bobby pin is attached as in Figure 1. Lay the rope on your table or a chair.

To Load: To attach the card to the gimmick, first pick up the loop at point A with your left hand. The card is palmed in your right hand, and as your right hand reaches the gimmick, the card slips naturally under it and is held there firmly.

Still holding the rope with your right hand, let go with your left and take the rope up again at point C. By pulling the rope you close the loop around your right hand and the card. Don't close it too tightly; leave a loop of about eight inches. Continue wrapping the rope around your hand until you reach the end, point D. This end is held between your right thumb and first finger as in Figure 2.

When the cards are thrown, toss the coiled rope, straightening your fingers. Hold on to the end with your thumb. As the lariat reaches its full length, a short jerk on the rope will close the noose around the card.

Presentation 1. Have a card in your right trouser pocket. Force a duplicate of this card, then let the spectator shuffle the deck. While this is being done, your right hand gets the card from the pocket and the left hand picks up the rope. The card is loaded into the gimmick as explained above. Finish the trick as described.

Presentation 2. Have the card in the gimmick at the start. The rope is coiled on your table. Force the card and during the shuffling pick up the coiled rope. Your hand naturally conceals the card. Conclude the feat in the usual way.

Presentation 3. No duplicates are used in this version. Use any deck. Have the spectator mark his freely selected card. After the card has been returned to the deck, palm it out and give him the deck

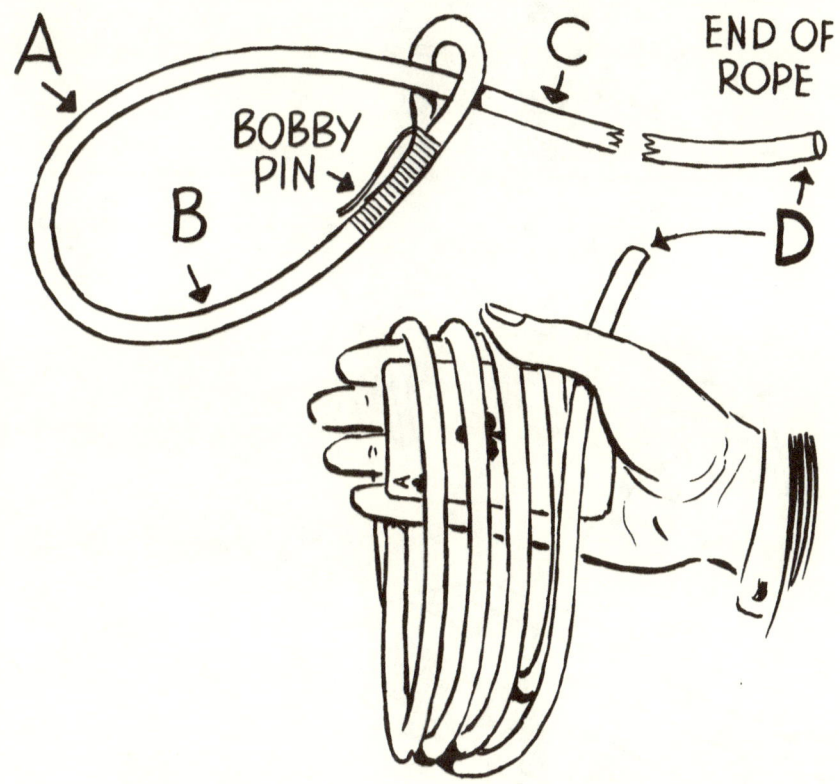

to be shuffled. Slip the palmed card in the gimmick when you pick up the rope. The spectator tosses the deck skyward; you throw your lasso. You snare the marked card in the noose.

The Devil's Flight

By Joseph Dunninger

A plank and two wooden saw horses are brought into view. The plank is placed upon the horses so that an improvised table is formed. A lady stands on the plank. She is covered with a cloth that doesn't reach to the stage. A pistol is fired; the cloth drops; the lady has vanished. This is one of the few illusions that can be worked on any stage without the use of traps and other such necessities that are usually employed to produce a similar effect.

Explanation: The saw horses are ordinary. The plank is prepared by attaching a cloth of the same color as the background used to its rear edge. A long, thin iron bar, which acts as a weight and also

CLOTH
ATTACHED
TO PLANK
SAME COLOR AS
BACK CURTAIN

STICK WITH
BALL ATTACHED

BACK CURTAIN →

← CLOTH
← ROD

enables the performer to roll up the cloth more easily, is sewn to the bottom of the cloth.

Before covering the girl, hold the cloth in front of the plank for a moment, during which time the girl releases the curtain with her foot. The bar attached to the cloth causes it to unroll. Under cover of the cloth the girl gets behind the masking curtain and holds up a stick with a ball attached to its end. This, when draped, causes the audience to believe the girl is under the cloth.

A shot is fired; the girl quickly pulls the stick out of view; the cloth falls, and the girl has vanished.

This illusion is very inexpensive to make, and a very effective finale. It is advisable to have a carpet of the same color and material as the background underneath the horses on the stage.

Is This Your Card

By Paul LePaul

You can't have too many methods for producing a chosen card. Here is one that I have found to be very useful, amusing and effective. It is one of those startling little effects that takes your audience by surprise.

The magician offers a spectator a free choice of one card from the deck. The spectator looks at the card, and is asked to remember it and replace it in the pack. Without the spectator's knowledge that you have done so, bring the card second from the top. The pack is then squared up in the left hand, taken with the right hand, as in Figure 1, and the bottom card is shown. The spectator is asked: "Is this your card?"

Upon his denial, the pack is returned face down to the left hand,

and the right hand, still in the same position, picks up the top card and by a turn of the wrist shows the face of the card as you ask if this is the chosen card. As this card is shown, the back of the right hand is rested on top of the deck. The thumb of the left hand secretly pushes out the second card, and the corner away from the body of the performer is grasped between the knuckles of the first and second fingers of the right hand, as in Figure 2. When the spectator denies that this is his card, the card is returned to the deck by turning the wrist as before, but naturally in the opposite direction. This automatically brings the chosen card sticking up between the first two fingers of the right hand facing the spectator. The magician then says, as he picks up the remainder of the pack with his right hand, "Then this must be your card."

The Miser's Dream As I Do It

By T. Nelson Downs

Of the many feats of magic, the so-called Miser's Dream or Aerial Treasury has always been my favorite, and with it I have been able to achieve an international reputation. Needless to say, the basic idea of this conjuring classic is very old and has been performed countless ways by countless scores of artists for a hundred years or more.

My own success in connection with the trick has been the result of a certain style of presentation, plus certain sleights and moves of my own origination. Many of these later are described for the first time in this article and it will be interesting for the reader to compare it with the original descriptions to be found in my book: "Modern Coin Manipulation." Time brings improvement.

Properties and preparation: I use about thirty-six half-dollar size palming coins. I prefer the usual Roterberg coin and find it advisable to smooth them by rubbing on a piece of carborundum. Also used is the familiar Kellar coin producer or holder, obtainable from all dealers. Remove the metal clip as it is not needed. The only other item is a hat. This I sometimes borrow, but more frequently I use a folding opera hat, to the bottom of which, on the inside, is riveted a circular piece of thin brass painted dead black. This, acting as a sounding board, materially increases the sound of the dropping coins.

The Kellar holder, loaded with about twenty coins, is placed in my right trouser pocket. In the left trouser pocket are the remaining coins.

Presentation: I pick up the folded opera hat and show it in my left hand. Right hand nonchalantly goes into my pocket and palms out the loaded holder. The hat is transferred to my right hand and snapped open by hitting it against the palm of the left hand.

The holder is held clipped under the edge of the brim, which enables me to display the interior of the hat and also my left hand. The hat, together with the holder, is transferred to the left hand and the right is displayed. This is repeated whilst making introductory remarks. This freedom in handling the hat and the load is only made possible by using the Kellar holder.

Finally, the holder is clipped by the left fingers inside the hat against the sweatband in the approved position. The production now commences. The right hand reaches into the air and pretends to catch a coin, which is apparently tossed into the hat. Simultaneously, a coin is released from the holder with the left forefinger. I remove a coin from the hat, display and then apparently toss it back. In reality, of course, the coin is palmed and another coin is released from the holder.

I shall not go into a detailed description of the catching procedure as it is familiar to all. The secret, of course, is to vary the operation as much as possible and, above all, to dramatize it to the fullest extent.

I will, however, submit a couple of original wrinkles that greatly enhance the production. As a coin is released from the holder sharply lift the hat upward a few inches. This greatly increases the impact of the coin and greater sound results. Another move I use to secure the same result is this: After producing a palmed coin at the fingertips, deliberately throw it with considerable force into the hat. As the coin leaves the fingers, the hand must be almost out of sight in the hat so that, when the coin hits, the left hand releases another one from the holder which is forthwith palmed in the right hand in readiness for production. I do this intermittently through the routine and find that it puzzles people who know a thing or two. This sleight requires timing but is simple enough to learn easily.

To vary the production as much as possible I, of course, pass a coin through the bottom of the hat. That is very old business but my method is a bit different. I hold the coin against the hat and between the first finger and thumb. Now exerting a slight pressure causes the coin to swing on a pivot, so to speak, and out of sight behind the fingers. By all means try this simple move in front of a mirror to appreciate its singular illusion.

Another familiar and effective move is apparently to toss a coin high into the air and, a second later, catch it in the hat as it makes an inivisible descent. Here again, my procedure is a bit different. The coin, as usual, is tossed into the air (really palmed) and the hat is held out in readiness to receive it. However, after a brief wait, the coin does not appear. I look at the audience puzzled. Then I turn my head right, still looking for it. At this point a coin is released and when it "hits", I turn and look at the hat in great surprise. Properly timed, this is a sure laugh.

By now I have produced about twenty coins in as varied a manner as possible. I start quite slowly and del'berately but gradually increase the tempo. I now introduce one of my favorite creations, the production of any number of coins called for at my fingertips. I stall a bit by talking and my left hand goes into the hat deliberately, palms out about sixteen coins and holds them clipped against the sweatband. I show my right hand and transfer the hat, but the sixteen coins (more or less) remain palmed in the right hand.

Suppose I am asked to produce eighteen coins—this is two more than I have palmed, but it doesn't matter. The coins are palmed overlapping a bit and are produced one at a time in a fan held between the first fingers and thumb. Proceed as follows: The third finger pulls away one coin from the rest and assisted by the second finger brings it into view between the first finger and thumb. This is repeated so that the second coin suddenly joins the first with a noisy "clink." This is repeated with the remainder. It requires a very considerable degree of practice to do this neatly but, as the old saying goes, the student will be amply repaid for his labors.

As stated above, if you have only, say, sixteen coins palmed and are required to produce eighteen, it doesn't matter. I bridge the difficulty by simply pretending to catch two coins at intervals and make the illusion perfect by snapping one of the coins already produced with the third finger. The extra sound is there even if the extra coin is not. At the conclusion of the production, I am holding a fan of coins between my thumb and first finger of the right hand. I now drop them singly into the hat, counting aloud as I do so. If I am "short" a few, a gesture is made of dropping them and simultaneously the right number are released singly from the left hand. This, properly done, is quite indetectable.

After the above, whenever time permits, I make a trip into the audience catching coins from their "whiskers" and elsewhere. As I step into the audience, I deliberately palm out the additional load of coins from the left trouser pocket so that I'm all set. While in the midst of the audience, I brazenly steal handfuls of coins from the hat and shake them from spectators' handkerchiefs, neckties, etc. To the average layman, this is the most marvelous part of the entire routine.

In any event I finish the trick by streaming a number of coins from a spectator's nose with the remark: "This gentleman always blows himself about this time of the evening."

My only purpose in writing this little article has been to reveal a few good things in connection with the grand old tricks which will never grow old.

The Triangular Room

By John Mulholland

The four Jacks from a pack of giant cards are shown to the audience. The magician also displays a thin triangular board. On the lower side of this board are three feet, one at each corner, and on the upper side, six double brackets, two on each side. The board is put on the table with the point of the triangle away from the audience. One of the Jacks is slid into the brackets in the board, and then the second Jack is also put in the brackets. At this point, the two cards form an angle with the open part of the "V" toward the audience. The third Jack is then put in the brackets at the front of the board, so as to make an enclosed triangular room of cards. The fourth Jack is then dropped on the top to make a ceiling. The base is given a quarter turn so that one of the angles points towards the audience, Figure 1. The magician makes his incantation, the roof card is removed and the magician produces a quantity of silks, etc., from the room of cards. So much for the effect.

As far as the base and the cards are concerned, they are exactly as they seem and completely unprepared. Figure 2 shows the construction of the base.

In order to better show the cards, the magician also has a skeleton easel. At the beginning of the trick, the four cards rest in a stack upon this easel, faces toward the audience, Figure 3. When the magician exhibits the cards, he takes one from the easel at a time and calls attention to the suit of each Jack. When he has reached the third Jack, he holds it with the other two previously shown, in a fan, and then without touching the fourth Jack, merely calls attention to its being the fourth suit. He then puts the three Jacks back on the easel, while showing the innocence of the wooden base.

Figure 4 shows the construction of the skeleton easel. The upright sticks of this easel, as well as the cross bar connecting them, are rabbetted out in a "v" shape groove to hold the cards. Also on the inner side of the uprights are saw slots running vertically. Figure 5 shows the top view of one of these uprights. The construction of the card and its triangular load is shown in Figure 6. The card is slightly narrower than the Jacks and just a little shorter. It is best made of thin fibre wood board. The container itself may be made of fibre board or a thin metal. The load compartment is half an inch narrower than the card and half an inch shorter than the height of the card. In order that the fourth Jack does not slip out of the easel before it should, there are two metal lips at the top edges of the easel which stick out toward the front exactly the thickness of the card, Figure 5 A. In order to make

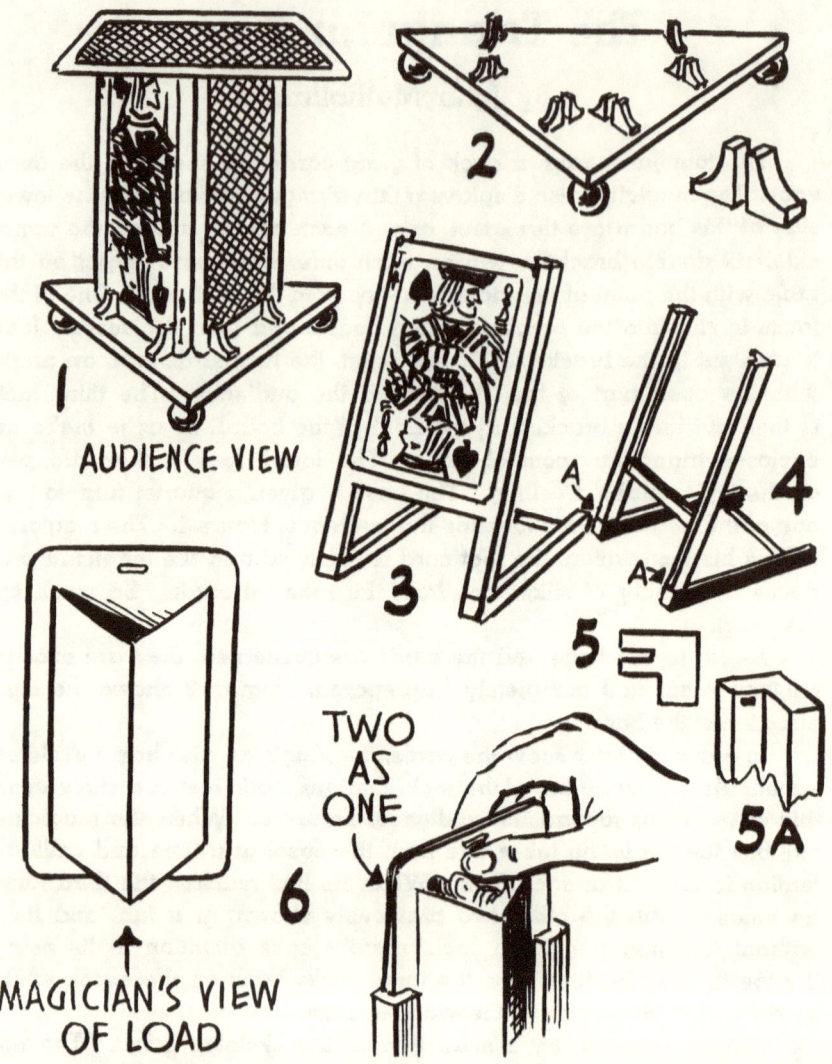

AUDIENCE VIEW

TWO AS ONE

MAGICIAN'S VIEW OF LOAD

packing easier, the uprights of the tripod are hinged to the base A-A in Figure 4.

In performing the trick the fourth Jack is left on the easel in order to mask the load at that time. When the Jacks are again picked up to put them in the brackets on the base, the first two Jacks are lifted straight up from the easel and casually put in the base. In lifting these Jacks from the easel, the fingers of the right hand are pressed against the top of the card. Friction will slide a card up until it can be grasped at the back with the thumb. The third card is lifted in the same manner, except that the thumb grasps the card with the load and pulls it up along with the third Jack. These two cards, as one, are then stuck in the base. Because of the lips the fourth Jack does not come out at the time the third Jack and the load are lifted. In picking up the fourth Jack, the thumb presses at the back and bends the Jack until the corners snap out from under the lips. It is then taken from the easel as were the first three, and dropped on top of the room of cards. As soon as this fourth Jack is taken, the easel is seen to be the lightest sort of skeleton, and it is inconceivable to the audience that it can play any part in the trick.

Due to the fact that the third Jack had been shown on both sides at one point in the trick, and merely slid off the fourth Jack when taken from the easel to build the room, there seems to the audience no possible way for a load to be introduced.

In making the load container, the apex of the triangle can be made to open, in order that it too will pack flat.

Diminishing Golf Ball Routine

By Ballantine

Ireland's diminishing golf ball effect is one of the smartest effects in modern manipulative magic. However, the routine worked out by Laurie Ireland has one defect for the night club performer—bad angles. People on the side or rear can see the gimmick as it extends from the hand. (See "Greater Magic", page 649.) I have worked out a method of handling the balls which enables the performer to work surrounded on all sides.

A colored silk is thrown over the left hand. The right hand holds the large ball at its fingertips. The gimmick is inside, Figure 1. The ball is placed on the silk and held through it by the fingertips of the left hand. The gimmick is underneath the ball, concealed by the silk, Figure 2. The right hand is cupped over the ball. Pretend to squeeze it, but really palm it off. At this instant, the left hand turns over, allowing the silk to hang so that it conceals the gimmick, Figure 3. Run the right hand down the silk several times, stating that you have caused the ball to diminish in size.

The left hand turns upright again to its original position, permitting the silk to fall away and reveal the large end of the dumbbell gimmick, Figure 4. The right hand goes to the pocket and brings out the palmed ball in order to compare its size with that of the diminished ball. Replace the large ball in the pocket.

The left hand again turns over. As it does the left fingers reverse the ends of the dumbbell. The right hand strokes the silks several

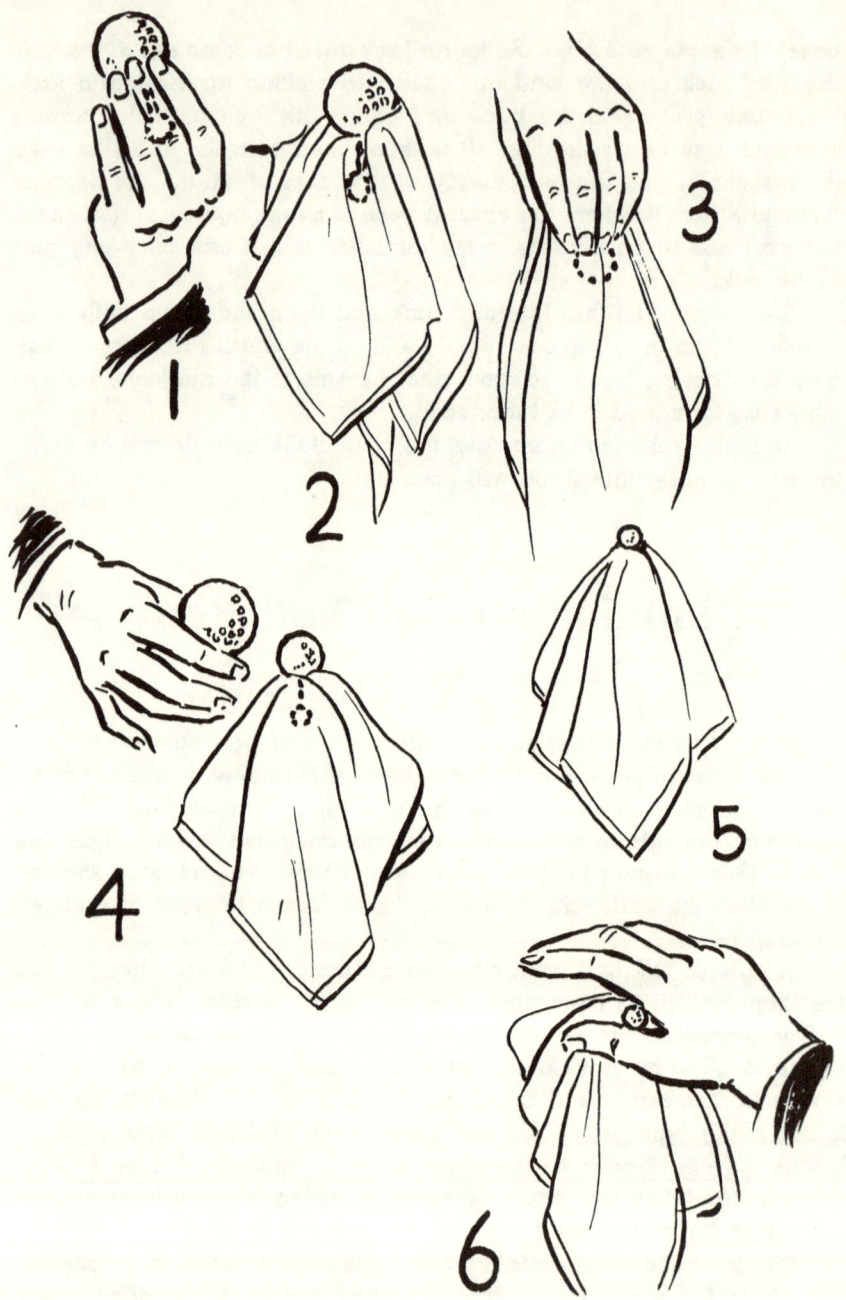

times, then the left hand turns back to its original position. The silk
falls away and reveals the small ball, Figure 5. The large ball is
again brought out for comparison, then replaced. The right hand now
grasps the edge of the silk nearest the audience and folds it back over

the small ball. As it passes over the ball, the gimmick is thumb palmed. The right hand goes to the pocket, leaves the gimmick and brings out the large ball to compare it with the ball which, apparently, is still in the silk.

The left hand shakes the silk open, holding it by one corner, to show that the ball has vanished. Remark that the ball is now so small that it is invisible.

Get the Point?

By Arthur Leroy

I've been keeping this effect for my own use and never intended to release it. However, I noticed an advertisement a short time ago offering a like effect for sale at a dollar. As I've been showing it to magicians around New York for the past eight years, I figure it's time to let it out and get it over with. I just mention the affair to keep from being accused of pirating my own effect.

The effect is simple but cute. A card is selected, returned to the deck and is lost in the shuffle as usual. Then the pack is balanced on the blade of a standard, flat, table knife. The pack is thrown from the blade and, as the cards fall, the knife is wielded in the air among the cards. Wonder of wonders—ta-ran-ta-ran-ta-ran-to-ra—the selected card is seen impaled on the knife.

Cut a slit through the mid-section of a court card just a bit wider than a table knife blade. That's all the preparation you need.

Force this card by any method that gives the spectator a sight of the card but doesn't necessitate its removal from the pack. After the card has been noted, bring it to the top, false shuffle leaving it on top, and all is in readiness. Hoosah.

Turn the pack face up, and, at the same time, separate the slit card from the rest of the pack just a trifle with your little finger. In placing the knife, run it between the slit card and the deck so that it passes through the slit and out on the far side. The slit card is now impaled and all that remains is to throw the deck in the air, stab, and there, sir, is your card. Keep your index finger on the card while stabbing, so that the momentum doesn't dislodge it from the blade. After a couple of tries you'll find it quite easy to insert the blade properly without any trouble. Try it out. As you can see, its effect upon a layman is tremendous, since you can use a borrowed knife and a borrowed deck, preparing the slit in an instant while you are performing some out-of-the-room stunt prior to this one. Carry a sharp razor blade and you will attain a far greater effect than you possibly could with an expensive Card Dagger or Card Sword.

Penetration Most Extraordinary

By Tan Hock Chuan

Into a glass tumbler are put three colored silks, brown, green and blue. The blue silk is put in first with the others on top. A lady's handkerchief is put over the tumbler and secured around its mouth with a rubber band.

Pinching at the bottom of the tumbler, the magician pulls out the blue silk, which is seen to leave the tumbler gradually. The tumbler is left intact with the lady's handkerchief, the rubber band and the two other silks undisturbed.

Method: A black thread is attached to one corner of the blue silk. Shove the blue silk into the tumbler first, leaving the thread over the

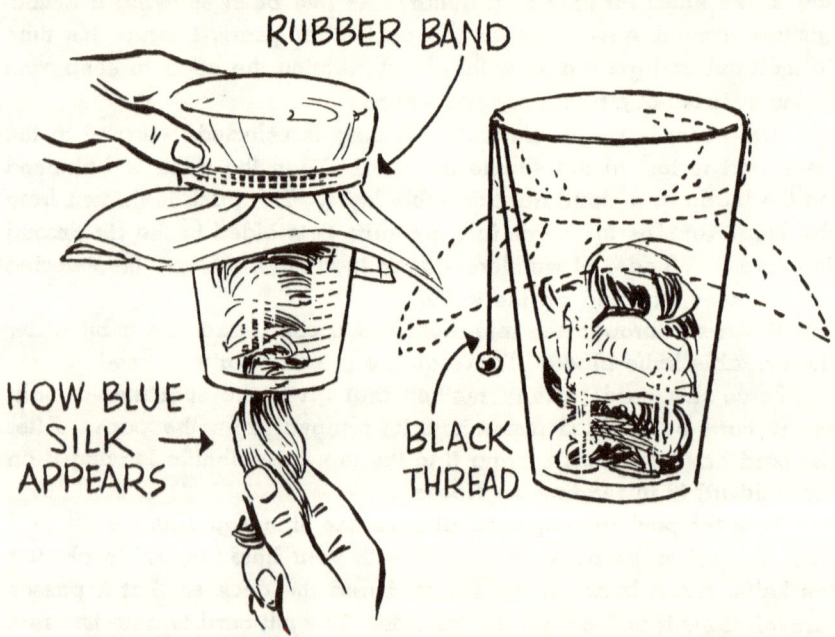

RUBBER BAND

HOW BLUE SILK → APPEARS

BLACK THREAD

edge and hanging down. On top of the blue, put in the other two silks. Put the lady's handkerchief over the mouth of the tumbler and fasten it in place with the rubber band.

Hold the tumbler so that the left hand is around the lower end. Show it on all sides. Then with the right hand, make a series of pulls on the thread until the corner of the blue silk appears below the tumbler. Then pull it slowly. The illusion that the silk is emerging directly through the glass is uncanny. Pull the blue handkerchief completely out. It is strange that the silk can leave the tumbler with the elastic band and covering handkerchief still intact.

Silk Penetration

By Mohammed Bey (S. Leo Horowitz)

Here is a silk penetration effect that involves neither fakes nor prepared silks. It is an adaptation of the pencil or cigar through silk effect. (Seymour Davis: "Phantom Hanky," Feb., 1939, p. 317.) In the following version, the effect has more visual appeal as it is, of

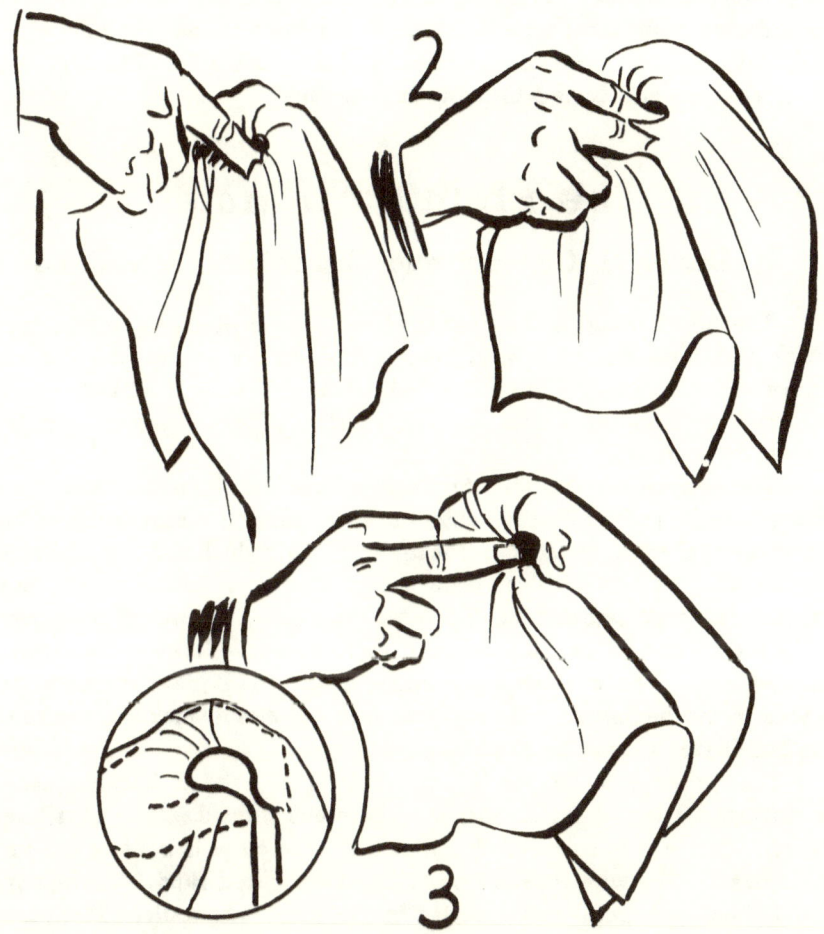

course, more colorful. A dark silk is spread over the left fist and a depression is made in the center of the silk. A second silk of a light, contrasting color is pushed into the depression of the first silk. A corner of the light silk suddenly appears from the underside of the dark silk. The right hand reaches under and pulls this end down a bit, then it reaches back and pulls the top end. After pulling the light silk back and forth a few times it is eventually pulled clear of the dark silk. Both silks may be examined; they are free from damage.

Method: This is identical with the earlier idea. The first silk is spread over the left fist. The right forefinger starts the depression and begins a twisting motion. In this motion the back of the hand would first be facing the ceiling, then the palm would be up, Figure 1. During the action the second finger comes alongside of the index finger, the index finger slips out and bends back, and the second finger continues the twisting motion, Figure 2. However, when the second finger is withdrawn a moment later a channel has been made through which the light silk can pass on the outside of the dark silk. The light silk is pushed in and pulled through as described.

The Phantom Flame

By Carlos H. Colombi and Graciela N. Avendano

The effect about to be described requires a precisely made gimmick and a certain amount of presentation ability so that the various movements blend into an integrated whole. This is a trick that will astonish any audience and leave it without a logical explanation for what has occurred.

The magician lights the candle in a candlestick on his table. He takes it out of the candlestick with his left hand, and removes the white handkerchief from his breast pocket with his right hand. He covers the candle. A few magical passes and the flame and a part of the candle are seen penetrating the handkerchief. The magician shows the covered candle on all sides and lights a cigarette from the flame. Immediately he pulls away the handkerchief. The lighted candle is as it was in the beginning. He replaces it in the candlestick. If desired, the handkerchief may be examined.

The gimmick is simple to construct. You need a 10-inch piece of galvanized iron wire, no larger in diameter than the lead of a fine pencil. One end is soldered to a thumb tip, the other is bent as shown in Figure 1. The wire must be perfectly straight and rigid. The upper end is filed to a point and inserted into a piece of candle. The wire is painted dead white. The thumb tip is the usual flesh color. Also needed is a brass tube of the exact size of a common candle, some 12 inches long, the diameter of which will permit the end of the wire to fit neatly in cut as shown in Figure 2. The other end of the tube is closed, and the whole tube is painted dead white to simulate a candle. The candle end, pierced by the sharp end of the wire, is inserted in the cut-out top of the tube so that the thumb tip lies at the

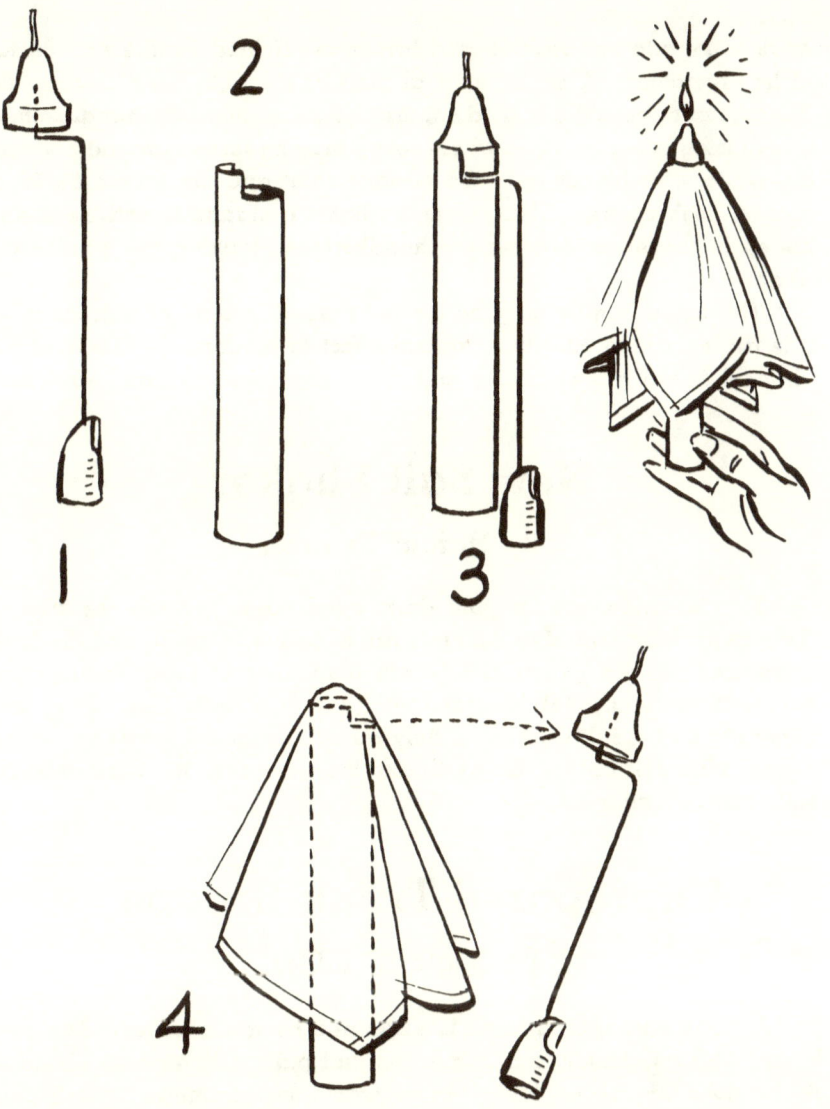

base of the pseudo candle. The audience sees what appears to be just a candle in a candlestick.

Presentation: The magician takes the lighted candle from the candlestick with his right hand holding the candle and wire together. Passing it to his left hand, he inserts his left thumb into the thumb tip. The right hand removes the pocket handkerchief and displays it in front of the candle. At this precise moment the left thumb moves back and takes with it the wire to which the candle end is attached. The left hand doesn't move, only the thumb. The right hand covers the action, then places the handkerchief over the candle. The left thumb moves back to its original position and brings the lighted candle end on top of handkerchief. A slight magical pass of the right hand covers this. The audience sees the lighted candle end penetrating the handkerchief. The illusion is perfect. The whole set-up may be turned around because the white wire blends with the handkerchief and the thumb tip is, of course, flesh colored. The magician lights a cigarette, and, reversing his early moves, withdraws the handkerchief, leaving the candle still alight.

The faked candle may be made of wood instead of a brass tube. It is a pleasure to offer this original effect to readers of "The Sphinx." I hope they will have as much enjoyment in presenting it as I have had.

New Salt Shaker

By Harold Pearson

This is a new use for your drum head tube. Handle the tube in the regular way and after the ends are closed with tissue and the load is secured, take a pencil and punch a number of holes through the double tissue end. Ask someone what the tube looks like. They will generally say a salt shaker. If they do not, suggest it yourself. Have a dark blue silk on the table. Shake the tube over it. Sure enough, salt comes pouring out.

Unprepared Trunk Escape

By Louis N. Miller

A large unprepared trunk is examined by a committee. The performer dresses himself in a large robe and pulls a mask over his face. As he does this, he explains that he wants the committee to lock and rope the trunk after he is placed inside. He brings forward a screen which he stands behind the trunk, then he gets in the trunk and the men from the audience proceed to lock and tie it with ropes.

Suddenly the performer comes running down the theatre aisle. The committee opens the trunk. Out steps a lady in evening dress.

Solution: The secret lies in a quick change made when the performer steps behind the screen to bring it forward. The screen stands to the left of the stage as far back as possible and close to the wings. The lady assistant dressed in matching robe and mask is behind it. The instant the performer steps behind the screen, the lady comes forward. In picking up the screen from the front, she brings it close enough to the wings so that the performer will be hidden as he dashes off stage.

The screen is then brought to the trunk. The masked figure gets inside the trunk, and quickly removes her robe and mask when the lid is closed. Meanwhile the performer has run to the front of the theatre, where he waits for the logical moment to run down the aisle.

As any trunk will do you can safely offer a reward for anyone who can show that it is prepared in any way. In fact, you can borrow a trunk in each city.

The Cut and Restored Cigarette

By Charles W. Fricke

The performer opens a pack of cigarettes, removes one and puts the package back in his pocket or on the table. With a pair of scissors he cuts the cigarette in two in the middle. He shows the cigarette freely and allows the audience to see his hands are empty. With one half of the cigarette in each hand, he brings his hands together, shows the cigarette suddenly restored and lights and smokes it.

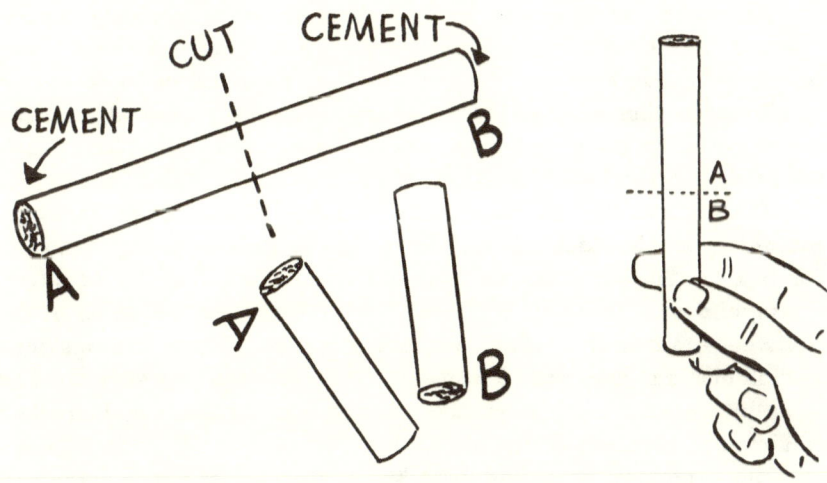

Explanation: The ends of the cigarette are first treated with one of the good rope cements. Care must be taken that the entire edge of the paper is coated. When the cigarette is cut, the treated ends are put together between your hands. The joint is so nearly air-tight that the cigarette can be smoked.

Coin in Ball of Wool Idea

By Herb Runge

Have the ball of wool, with the coin slide in it in a paper sack. The fake is sticking out of the sack on the side away from the audience.

When you steal the marked coin from your rattle box or from under a handkerchief, secretly insert it in the slide as you pick up the bag.

Reach in and remove the ball of wool with your right hand. Your left hand retains the slide in the sack by pressure on the sides.

All that remains is to have the wool unwound. The marked coin is inside.

Harbin's Production Box

By Robert Harbin

There must have been thousands of production boxes invented, but here is one which is different—and deceiving. More important, it holds an enormous quantity of silk.

An elongated box with no bottom is shown completely empty; a wand is pushed through holes in the top and sides when the box is facing the audience, as in Figure 4. Nothing could be more empty.

Then, as illustrated—Figure 1—large silks are produced from the the holes in the sides and from inside. There is no hesitation. They are produced at once.

The construction is cheap and simple. Figure 2 is the secre. container, which slides up and down and is stopped in the center of the box by the stops shown in figure 3. The holes in the container correspond with those in the outer case. There are six holes in the container—four in the sides, two in the bottom. These are one inch in diameter and are closed with two strips of elastic as shown. The holes in the outer case have star traps made of rubber and are one and one-half inches in diameter.

The container, or sliding box, has a piece of one inch tubing in the center so that a wand or stick can be thrust through when the box is shown to be empty. When the box is inverted, the first finger prevents the sliding section from falling into place until the right moment.

Each silk has a black bottom sewn to a corner which makes it easy to get at through the star traps. The silks are loaded from the outside so that the buttons are flush against the elastics in the

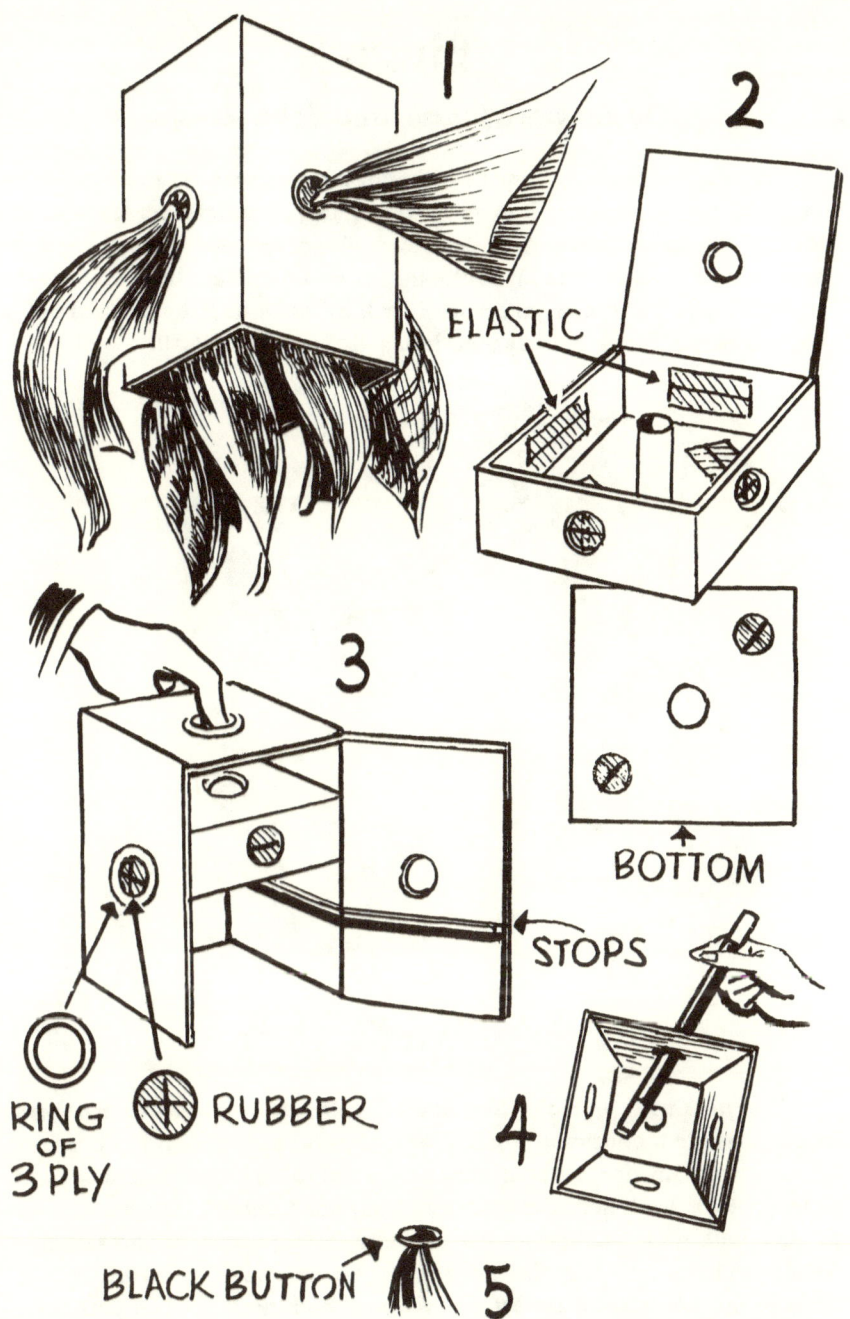

1

2

ELASTIC

BOTTOM

3

STOPS

RING
OF
3 PLY

RUBBER

4

BLACK BUTTON 5

container, which hold them in position. The interior of the box is painted black. The outside is coated with any desired color and with any pleasing decoration.

Bingo

By Stewart Judah and John Braun

Bingo, the modern version of Lotto, has become so popular in the last few years that it is known in every city, hamlet and town in the land. The mere mention of the word Bingo arouses interest, and for that reason we have used it as the title of an interesting little trick for the club or stage performer, although it will be seen that the trick about to be described bears little resemblance to the game itself.

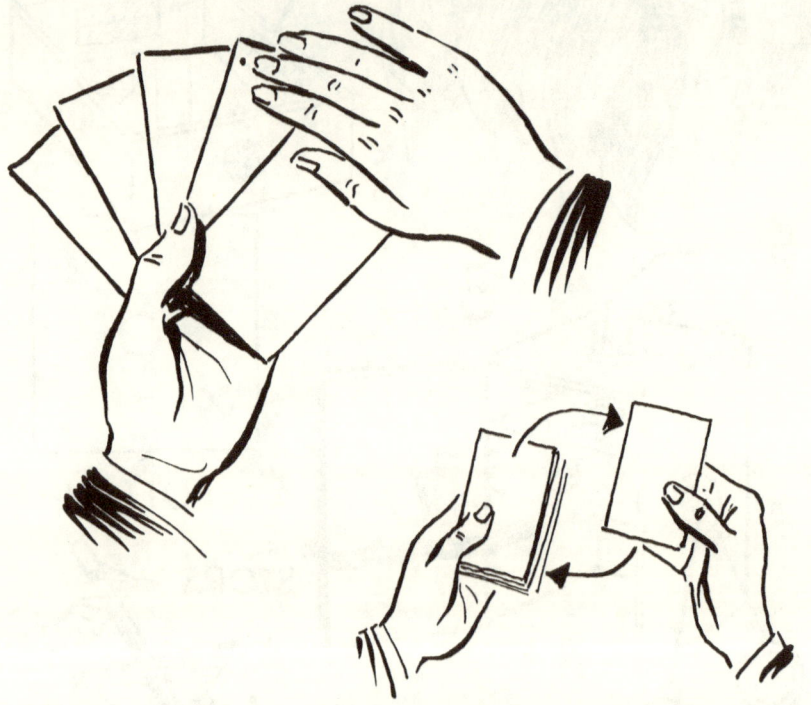

The performer exhibits five sealed coin, or pay, envelopes, and hands them to a spectator to mix thoroughly. Taking them back again, he explains that one of them contains a valuable prize, and this prize is to go to the winner of a game of simplified Bingo, that he intends to play with four spectators. He explains that the word Bingo has five letters and, as he holds the envelopes, he proposes to award one to each of the four spectators by a process of elimination. The performer himself will keep the last envelope. He says that he will spell Bingo, transferring an envelope from top to bottom of the stack for each letter, and award the envelope at the last letter to the first spectator. This spelling process is to be repeated until but one envelope remains, which he will retain. The spelling begins as the performer stresses that the envelopes were mixed by a member of the audience. In fair and deliberate fashion each of the four spectators now get an envelope. Each spectator opens his envelope and finds inside a slip of folded newspaper or the performer's business card. The magician, good honest man, finds a crisp $20 bill in his envelope.

Five coin envelopes are needed. One is marked with a pencil dot in the upper left hand and lower right hand corners of both sides, so that after the mixing, the performer can locate it at a glance. Seal a $20 bill in this envelope. In each of the others seal a folded piece of newspaper the size of a bill, or a business card or advertising piece.

Come forward with the envelopes. Have a spectator mix them. When you take them back, hold them fanned in the left hand and locate the marked envelope. This must be brought second from the top before you begin spelling. This can be easily accomplished by a shuffle, or cut, while explaining the rules and conditions of the game. If this is not done, your money is lost. We wouldn't want that to happen. Step up to the first spectator, spell and transfer an envelope from top to bottom with each letter. Hand the envelope, at the letter O to the spectator. Repeat this with the other three spectators. Keep the last envelope yourself. If you have made no mistakes, you will hold the marked .envelope. When the ends are torn away, the performer will be the winner and a gasp of surprise will be heard when the spectators see the valuable prize.

The Secret Panel

By Herman L. Weber

Hocus Pocus! And what will you have? A new flower growth? A sensational duck vanish? A really mysterious production of a stack of bowls? A new appearing, exchanging or vanishing girl illusion? A bewildering production screen? These and many more are here for you in the Secret Panel.

A two-panel screen painted, say, red on two sides and green on the other two, is shown on all four sides to be solid and unprepared. Despite this a load of large proportions is concealed.

One glance at the drawing reveals all. There is a secret panel, without legs, that is hinged to, and hangs behind, the screen at all times. This panel supports a shelf for bowls, ducks or what you will. Opposite it on the right, the panel contains two secret doors, held flat by spring hinges. These doors open only one way so the inside back of the panel has a small moulding to hold them when they are rapped to prove their solidity.

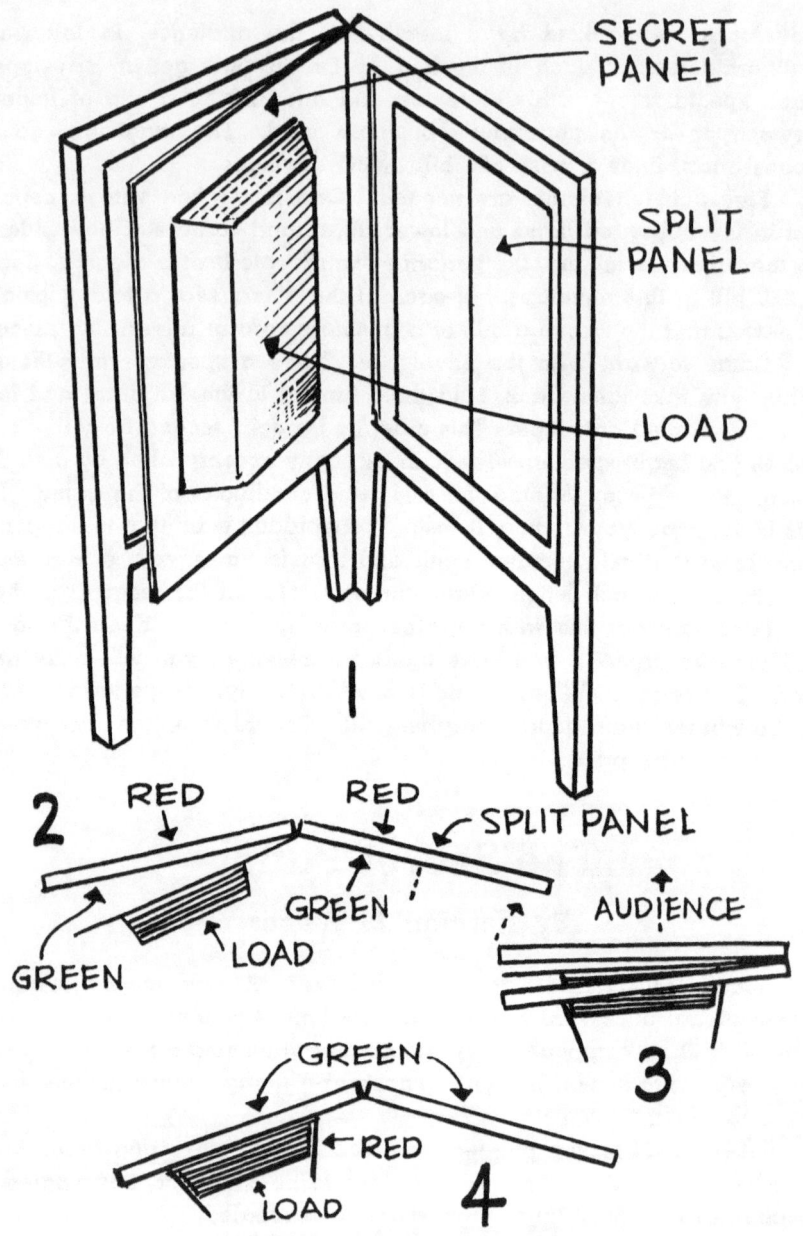

SECRET PANEL

SPLIT PANEL

LOAD

1

2 RED   RED   SPLIT PANEL

GREEN

GREEN   LOAD

AUDIENCE

3

GREEN

RED

LOAD   4

The manipulation of the screen is simple and direct. The performer stands behind the screen, leans over and raps the front panels with wand or knuckles. The split panel is then brought to the back toward the performer and onto the other panel. It is knocked against the back of the other panel and that panel is opened out so that the other two sides are brought into view.

In reality, however, when the split panel slaps against the secret panel, its doors open to allow the load to pass through. Thus when the solid front panel is opened forward, the other side of the load panel which is flat and solid now faces the audience in place of the unseen section of the split panel.

The color contrast between the red front panels and the green back panels makes it apparent that the screen has been shown on all sides.

Jasonism

By Eddie Joseph

It is a well-known psychological axiom that an effect only appears supernatural when the true cause escapes us. I provide such an example in Jasonism. I held this in reserve 15 years, using it sparingly, only on special occasions, to great advantage. The direct approach and absence of "out of sight action" convince the close observer that trickery does not play a part.

The performer remarks that he is about to present a brief, but convincing, exhibition of thought reading. Instead of the usual blindfold, he asks one of the men to stand behind him and place his hands over the operator's eyes. The second man is requested to shuffle either his own or the performer's cards. Then he is told to cut the pack and place one portion on the performer's outstretched hand. The remainder of the pack is discarded.

The performer shows the cards, one at a time, and asks the gentleman to make a mental record of one card and its position in the pack. While showing the cards, the performer continues: "In order to make sure that I cannot gain the slightest clue which may eventually lead me to your selection, please do not stop me as soon as you decide on a card but let me continue right through."

Thus the operator shows the face of every card and points out that since the selection is made mentally no one but the selector can identify it.

"But," adds the performer, "if we could bring our minds in agreement I would be able, with remarkable certainty, to probe into the innermost recesses of your mind and share your secret."

The packet is handed to the gentleman with the explanation that the only way to bring two minds into agreement is to raise one to an active state, to lower the other to a passive state. Since the performer is to read the other's mind, the gentleman is instructed to raise his mind to a state of activity, by concentrating intently on the card and its original position. He is warned that success depends entirely upon his concentration because thought reading is not a one-sided matter. As an untrained mind cannot concentrate on two things, the man is asked to form a mental image of his selected card and bring in artificial aid by transferring one card at a time from the top of the packet to the bottom to equal the position at which his card stood originally. Then the gentleman is instructed to call out the names of every card in his hands. No sooner is this done than the performer intercepts the mental vibrations and names the card.

A careful analysis will satisfy the reader that the strongest point of Jasonism is its simplicity. The "cause" will definitely evade the keenest observer due to that simplicity. Since the observer feels that the performer is ignorant of the identity of the card and does not restrict the number of cards employed, the investigating witness is robbed of a starting point.

We shall now investigate the "cause." After the group of cards is in the performer's hand, he announces that he will show the face of every card so that one may be mentally chosen and its position remembered. The performer pushes the top card over. His right hand takes it and holds it up. The next card is handled in the same manner, but it is placed in front of the card already in the right hand. This is continued. Each card goes in front of the preceding one. When 8 or 9 cards are shown, the performer drops the group in his right hand on the table and continues with the rest of the pack in the same manner. The entire success of the problem depends upon this innocent subterfuge.

However, the performer must remember the number of cards he drops on the table in the first lot. Suppose it is nine. He continues to count, to himself, right through in order to ascertain the total number of cards in the packet handed to him. Suppose this is twenty-three. He deducts nine from twenty-three, which leaves fourteen. He must remember this number.

A reason is given in the patter for transferring a certain number of cards from top to bottom. Suppose the gentleman concentrated on the Jack of Diamonds, which happened to be in the eighth position. He will naturally move eight cards from top to bottom. You are not concerned with the original position of the card. As soon as he transfers the number of cards to equal the original position, he automatically places the card in the fourteenth position. All you have to do is listen for the name of the fourteenth card. The rest is showmanship.

This is the formula. The total number of cards in the packet, minus the number of cards the performer drops on the table in the first batch, equals the key number.

The working is elastic. If the performer drops thirteen cards in the first batch and the packet consists of eighteen, then, of course, the selected card will appear in the fifth position. However, the performer continues right through the rest of the cards after the original batch and drops them on the first lot. The entire packet is passed to the assisting spectator.

The Fidgety Poker Chips

By Nelson C. Hahne

The performer exhibits three ordinary poker chips, which can be examined by the audience, and a flat wooden tube. This tube is about six and one-half inches long. The chips are of different colors, such as red, white and blue. They are allowed to fall through the tube several times previous to the experiment. Finally, one end of the tube is held shut by the fingers of one hand. The chips are inserted in the opposite end in this order: red, white and blue. If this were not magic, the chips would be in the same order when they were permitted to slide out the other end. But here again the impossible happens! When the chips emerge they appear blue, first, red second, and white last. When the principle is understood the above routine might be enlarged by further similar effects. Remember the chips are unprepared. The audience may look through the tube before and after the feat. The chips may be slid through the tube previous to and following the experiment. Can this be possible?

You will need four ordinary poker chips. One red, one white and two blues. The tube is prepared. This preparation is simple and cannot be detected by the audience. See the drawing. The opening of this flat tube is only large enough for one chip to slide through at a time. The tube should be about six and a quarter or, better, seven inches long. It should be painted black on the inside. On the inside, about three-quarters of an inch from one end, is an indentation which will hold one chip in the wall of the tube. This is where the extra blue chip is concealed. If the tube is black on the interior the audience cannot see this preparation. The extra blue chip is in this space before the experiment begins. This side of the tube is kept nearer the floor so that the chip will not close the opening of the slide or slip out of the end of the tube. When the other chips are inserted they slide right over the concealed chip.

After the chips have passed through the tube several times, the tube is turned over so that the concealed blue chip falls out of the indentation into the channel of the slide. The tube is held upright in the left hand, and the chips are put in the opening. Red first, then white

END VIEW OF SLIDE

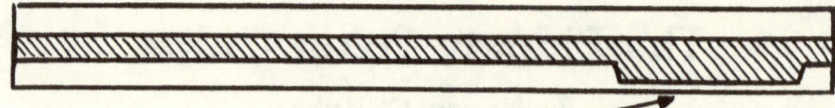

CONCEALED SPACE TO HOLD EXTRA
BLUE CHIP

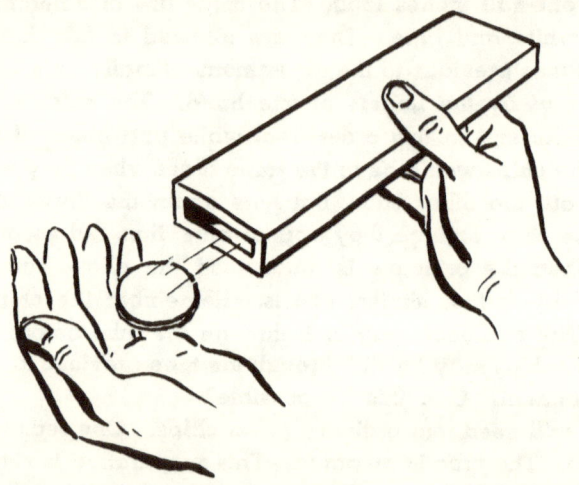

and blue. Now the tube is tilted so that the last blue chip falls into the cut-out space the other blue chip previously occupied. The chips are now allowed to slide out of the bottom. The impossible has been accomplished. Their order is changed.

The Waiter's Tip

By George DeMott

Eight small, individual size boxes of dry breakfast cereals—say, Corn Flakes, Shredded Wheat, Post Toasties, Wheaties, Bran Flakes, Puffed Rice and Kix—are in a row on the performer's table. A plate is also on the table. Five men are requested to hold coins aloft. One man, a penny; one, a quarter; one, a nickel; one, a dime, and the last, a half dollar. The performer asks a traveling man in the audience what he would consider a suitable tip for the waiter at breakfast. Suppose the man says a quarter. The magician instructs him to borrow the quarter from the man holding it. The other men are thanked and requested to put their coins back in their pockets.

The magician instructs the traveling man to mark the coin so that he positively will recognize it whenever he sees it. While this is done, the magician returns to the stage and gets a napkin. He wraps the quarter. It can be felt through the cloth. The traveling man selects his favorite of the eight cereals. The "waiter's tip" vanishes from the napkin. The top of the selected cereal is torn off and the breakfast food is emptied onto the plate. Along with the cereal the coin is seen to fall and heard to hit the plate. The box is ripped into pieces and discarded. The plate is passed to the traveling man. He verifies his mark on the coin. The coin is then returned to its owner.

Secret: A good sized slot is cut through the rear of each box on the side away from the audience. Backstage, in a row, are five napkins. Each has a coin of a different denomination sewn in the corner under an extra flap of cloth.

No matter which size coin is selected you have a gimmick ready for its vanish. The borrowed coin is palmed as the sewn-in coin is wrapped in the center. This is what is felt through the folds. Hold the napkin in the same hand that has the coin palmed to mask it.

Command the coin to vanish. Shake out the cloth, holding it by two top corners. Lay the napkin aside or put it in your pocket. The palmed coin is introduced into the selected box through the rear slot as you pick up the box to tear it open. Dump the cereal and the coin on the plate. Tear the box to bits and toss it away, thus no one can ever discover the slot.

The plate is handed to the traveling man, he identifies his mark on the quarter, then the coin is returned to its owner.

Your assistant, in the meantime, has removed the other boxes. If you work alone, you can put them in a shopping bag and set them aside, so that no one can find out about the slots. And there you have the mystery of "The Waiter's Tip."

A Tip for the Waiter's Tip

By Sid Lorraine

Personally, I'd have the five prepared napkins planted in various pockets. I'd have the plate in my inside coat pocket. It would get more laughs if you took the plate out of your pocket and also mention that you brought along a napkin from the Waldorf-Astoria.

I'd use eight unprepared boxes of cereal. While the coin is being marked, remove the plate and the required napkin. The coin is wrapped; the spectator feels the sewn-in coin through the cloth; you steal the marked coin.

Pick up the selected box of cereal. The fingers of the right hand press the coin against the back of the box. With your left hand, pull away the napkin from the spectator. The coin has vanished! Put the napkin aside and tear off the top of the box in your right hand. Start pouring the cereal. When about half is on the plate, release the coin. It will be seen to fall, apparently from the box, in the stream of breakfast food.

Step back and let the spectator verify the mark on the coin. Take your box and have the spectator return the coin to its owner. Meanwhile, pour the cereal back in the box and present it to your assistant for his kindness in helping. If you could produce a bottle of milk at this point, it would be a fitting climax.

I like the effect and think an audience will like it, too. George DeMott is to be congratulated for a novel clothing of the passing of a marked coin.

Silk Production Novelty

By Fred Mintz

Here is an extraordinary, smooth-working, little production effect which I am using in my act. It is a silk production from a magazine, which is shown freely on both sides, shaken and riffled to demonstrate that nothing is hidden between the pages. The magazine is rolled into a tube, the tube is shown to be empty, then four or more silks are produced from it. The magazine may be unrolled and shown at any time during the production, without disturbing or revealing the load. The trick is absolutely self-contained, requiring no body work, table loading, etc. Like it?

Here's the secret. The magazine, a thick one—I usually use "Cosmopolitan"—is prepared in this manner. Each of the inside pages is cut from a point at the back of the book, where the pages are joined, half way from the top to the bottom diagonally to the bottom at a point about four inches from the back. The cover is left intact. Spread a little glue around the cut edges of each page, close the book and let the glue dry.

Next take the cover from a duplicate magazine and glue it over the prepared magazine. As soon as the glue is dry, you are ready for your trick. You will have a magazine with a triangular compartment

PAGES ARE
CUT OUT
AS INDICATED

in it, capable of holding four or more silks. The reason for the di-
agonal section is that with it the magazine may be freely riffled to
show that it is empty.

The loaded magazine is held with the left hand covering the open end. The right hand riffles the pages. The magazine is rolled into a tube, and held with the compartment to the rear, so that the audience may look through the opening. Two silks are produced, the magazine is unrolled, shown, re-rolled, then the production continues.

Silver and Copper

By Paul N. Rylander

Three copper coins magically change places with three silver coins. The coins pass one at a time in the fairest possible manner. There are no suspicious moves for the sleights are covered by the necessary act of picking up the coins.

This routine will mystify, for it is done sufficiently slowly for the audience to think about it, yet no clue to the solution will be apparent.

Three half dollars are placed in a row on the left side of the table and three English pennies are placed parallel on the right. The coins form two lines extending from the magician to the spectators. Unknown to the audience, the magician has a gimmicked coin palmed in his right hand. This coin is a silver half dollar on one side and a copper English penny on the other. The coin is palmed with the half dollar side against the palm.

To begin the trick the magician uses his right forefinger to draw a mystic circle around the six coins. Then, using both hands, he slowly turns each coin over. With his left forefinger he traces another mystic circle around the coins in the opposite direction. This convinces the most observant spectator that faked coins, such as he has secretly palmed in his right hand, are not used.

The coin in the right hand is dropped to finger palm position in readiness for the key sleight upon which this feat is based. The left hand is extended, palm facing the audience, to receive the three coins which the right hand is about to place there.

The right hand, back to the audience, picks up a half dollar between the thumb and first finger and apparently lays it on the palm of the left hand. In reality it is switched for the gimmicked coin by bending the right forefinger a trifle to raise the half dollar above the gimmicked coin so that they will not clink as they pass. The fingers are tilted downward and, with a slight throwing motion not more than an inch or two, the gimmicked coin is slid off the fingers onto the left palm.

The right forefinger immediately lowers and the right thumb pushes the coin inward to the finger palm position. All this is the work of a second. It should look as if the half dollar were merely picked up and placed in the left palm.

Perhaps it is not exactly correct to say that the coin is in finger palm position. It really lies further forward on the fingers between the first and second joints. The further forward, the less motion is required in changing it.

The other two half dollars are put in the left palm in exactly the same manner—except that they are not exchanged. The three coins, over-lapping in a row, are fairly shown on the left palm, then the hand is closed slowly and turned over.

With the ordinary half dollar still lying on the tips of the fingers of the right hand, pick up the three copper coins with the forefinger and thumb. These are dropped on the half dollar so that when the hand is closed into a fist a copper coin is next to the palm ready to be palmed.

The two fists are knocked on the table. Without turning over the hands, open and push the coins onto the table, one from each hand simultaneously. If the left hand lays down its coins from the spectator to the performer, while the right hand lays the coins down in the opposite direction, each silver coin will have a copper coin opposite it, two copper and one silver coin on the left and two silver and one copper on the right. A copper coin is retained in the right palm.

The copper coin is dropped to finger palm position and once more the coins on the left are picked up. The gimmicked coin, copper side showing, is picked up first and switched for the ordinary copper coin as described earlier. It is well to have an identifying mark on both sides of the gimmicked coin so that it may be picked up without hesitation.

Next a silver coin is picked up and actually put in the left palm. The last silver coin is picked up and switched for the gimmicked coin by the above sleight. This time, however, it is necessary to reverse the gimmicked coin as it slides off the fingers. It is easily done by slanting the fingers of both the left and right hands a little more downward and tossing the coin with a trifle more force. The coin reverses when it hits the left fingers. The right hand completely hides the turnover. This move must not look any different than the other, and, indeed, if it is correctly done it does not. The copper coin, the gimmicked silver and the ordinary silver coins are freely displayed. The hand closes and reverses. The right hand, carrying a silver coin fingerpalmed, picks up the silver and two copper coins on the right with a copper coin on top so that it may be palmed when the hand is closed. The fists are knocked on the table, the fingers are opened and the coins slide onto the table two coins at a time, one from each hand. The spectators now see that there are two copper and one silver on the left and two silver and one copper on the right.

There is now but one copper and one silver to change places.

The copper, palmed in the right hand, is dropped to finger palm position. The right hand picks up the gimmicked copper and, in pretending to place it in the left hand, switches it for the ordinary copper coin. Then an ordinary copper is picked up and placed in the left hand. Finally the silver coin is picked up and switched for the gimmicked coin using the turn-over move. The coins in the left hand are stacked with the silver coin on top and held on the fingers. The hand remains open. The coins on the right are picked up so that the copper coin is on top. The pile is stacked evenly and held in the slightly cupped right fingers. Now comes a bold move. The right hand opens and turns over and displays the coins resting on the fingers. The coins are held as if they were about to be back palmed. Although there are three silver coins in this hand the audience cannot see them due to the slightly cupped position of the fingers. Both stacks of coins should be held in the same manner.

The performer extends his hands with a remark to the effect that there is but one copper and one silver left to change places. The hands are closed and turned over. The copper in the right hand is palmed and after the mystic pass, the coins are laid down showing all the copper now on the left and all the silver on the right.

The Hilliar Rising Cards

By William J. Hilliar

This is my original method for causing selected cards to rise from the deck in the left hand to the right hand held above it. I can stand in a drawing room with spectators all around me and move my position as often as desired.

The motive power is the piece of apparatus illustrated. It is a metal tube about eighteen inches long. By pulling the thread through the minute hole at the top, the weight rises naturally, but will fall again when the thread is loosened.

The weight should be about four times the weight of a playing card. The thread should be of the finest silk and should protrude from the apparatus about two feet when the weight rests at the bottom.

The apparatus must be pinned under your shirt, the hole on a level with your center shirt button hole, through which the thread is passed. To the end of the thread is attached a small pellet of wax, which is stuck on a vest button until ready for use.

Three cards are selected, returned and brought to the top of your pack. The waxed end of the thread is secretly attached to the back card. The right hand now passes all around the pack and, catching the thread between the first and second fingers, raises upwards.

The performer asks the name of the first card, and, upon being told, releases his left thumb pressure from the back card, which ascends immediately to the right hand. The fall of the weight in the tube causes this to happen.

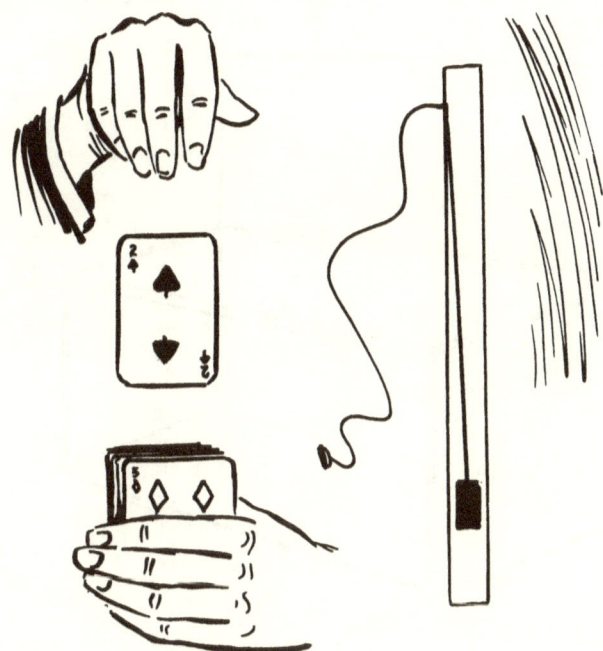

The card is then placed on the front of the pack. In so doing, the waxed thread is secretly removed and attached to the back card. The experiment is repeated with the two other selected cards.

By reading the foregoing carefully my readers will appreciate the superiority of this method, as the cards rise without the slightest movement of the performer and the thread is absolutely invisible even at close quarters.

A Magician's Hope Chest

By U. F. Grant

The magician calls attention to a box which he says is his "Hope Chest." The front and top doors are opened and it is obvious that the box is empty. The doors are closed. The performer says that he carries his toilet articles in the box when he travels. He opens the top door and produces a comb, brush, razor, shaving mug, shoe horn, necktie, collars, etc.

The box is shown empty again. The magician states that on his most recent trip around the world he saw a beautiful meadow with a brook running through it in England. He liked it so well that he put it in his Hope Chest and brought it home with him. He closes the box, then opens the top, reaches in and produces a picture of a meadow and a brook.

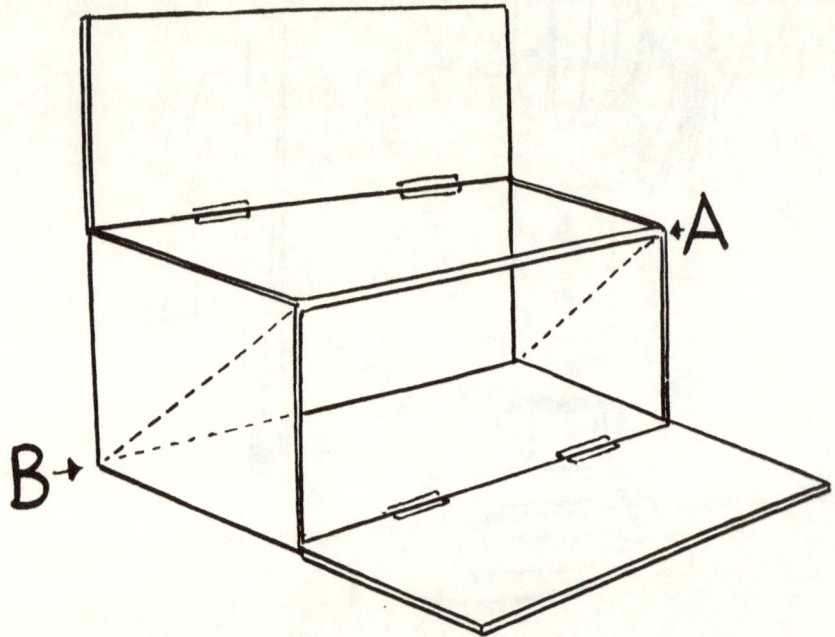

The magician continues that he has a pint of the bonded stuff in the box, but it is quite invisible. Before removing the liquid he passes the box out for examination. On its return he pours liquid out of the box into a bottle.

There is a mirror in the box running from the strip of wood A to the bottom of the back of the box B. A thin piece of nickel-plated brass makes the best mirror. The edges will not show if the box has a mahogany finish. Paste the picture to the back of the mirror with a strip of passe partout around the outside edge to form a frame. Both doors of the box should be opened at right angles. The reflection of the front door and hinges in the mirror makes it appear that you are seeing the back of the box, top door and hinges. The production articles are behind the mirror, and only the top door is open when they are produced. When the picture is produced, the back of the box is turned toward the audience. After this the box may be passed for examination.

To pour liquid from the box, use a bottle with a double funnel in the neck. Tilt the closed box, and apparently the liquid runs from the box through the funnel and into the bottle.

The Tennis Racquet Card

By H. Syril Dusenbury

This trick suggested itself to me when I was thinking of a way to improve the old fashioned card sword. Its effect is similar to that of the card sword, namely, a card is selected from the pack by a spectator

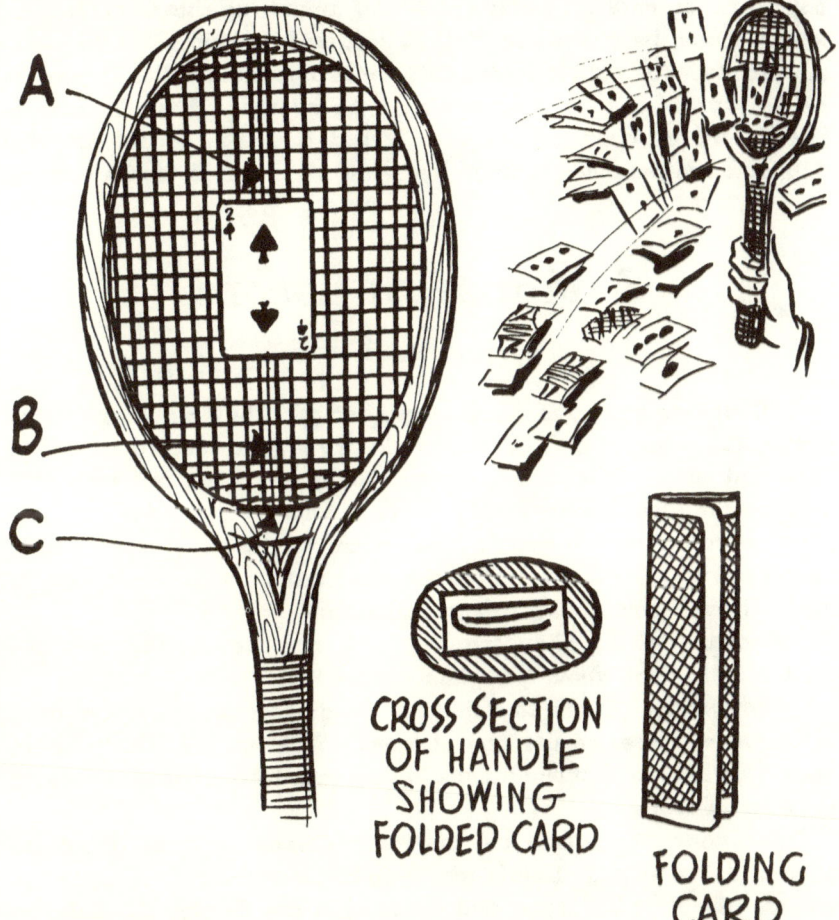

CROSS SECTION
OF HANDLE
SHOWING
FOLDED CARD

FOLDING
CARD

who notes what it is and returns it to the pack. The performer exhibits an ordinary looking tennis racquet and freely shows both sides to the audience. He requests the spectator who selected the card to throw the pack squarely at the racquet. When he does, all the cards but one fall to the floor. The chosen card is seen clinging to the strings of the racquet.

First of all, the card was forced. A duplicate is prepared like the old card in the bottle" card. It is cut in three parts and mounted on rubber hinges so that the card may be folded as shown in the illustration. The instant it is released it opens out flat.

The racquet must have a slot in the handle as shown at C. This is large enough to contain the folded card. A rubber cord, marked A, is fastened, as shown, to both the racquet and the card. This pulls the card from its hiding place at the proper time, and is invisible against the regular strings of the racquet. It is also necessary to fasten the bottom of the card to a piece of strong thread, as shown at B. The length should be gauged so that the card will be held in the center of the racquet. The card is folded and forced into the handle. It may be held by pressure over it, or a pin at the opening. After the card is forced and replaced, the deck is tossed and the racquet and the duplicate are permitted to jump into view as shown in the illustration.

A Matter of Record

By Judson Brown

"Doubtless you have heard people remark, 'As a matter of record, this is what I think!' or 'I think I should like to go on record as saying such and such.' Of course they don't really say 'such and such,' but you get the idea, and probably never having seen anyone put anything on record, for all you've heard them talk about it, you wonder how it's done. I'll show you. First, we must have a record, and to make it even better we'll use two of them."

A couple of flat phonograph records are shown. (Readers will please omit jokes about flat phonographs.)

"But we must have something to go on record. Here is a deck of cards—suppose we use one of them. Will you, sir, kindly select one? While I am shuffling it back in the pack, I would like the records to be examined."

The performer passes out the records, making jokes about the titles of the selections if he is that type of performer. Eventually the records are placed together and a pencil is run through the holes in the center of the records. They are then tied together and given to a spectator, who holds the pencil at either end, thus suspending the records between his hands. Another spectator holds the pack of cards. At command, a transposition takes place. The selected card vanishes from the deck and appears between the two records, impaled upon the pencil.

No duplicates are employed, hence a free selection of the cards is allowed and the selected card may be markd to prove the transposition is real as well as apparent.

The preparation consists in smearing some wax on the center of one side of one record. This is not put on as a pellet but spread on thin, and polished down, in which condition the record may be passed for examination without any danger of the wax being detected.

The card is selected and replaced. While the performer is busily engaged in recklessly shuffling the cards, while making sure the selected card remains on top, the records are passed for examination. The deck is put on the table. When the records are returned, the performer places them together so that the waxed side of the prepared record is on the outside, facing down. He lays the records on the table—and on the deck—while he borrows a pencil. When he picks up the records, he first presses down, which causes the top card to adhere to the wax. The records may be shown casually, as magicians show slates, then they are placed together with the card between the two. They are tied to prevent the card from being prematurely exposed to view. A sharp pencil is thrust through the holes, and the card, and then the spectator holds the ends of the pencil.

All properties are out of control of the performer. In spite of this he can still cause the transposition to take place, chiefly because it has already done so. The person who drew the card names it, the magician commands the passage to be made magically. The spectator with the pack finds that the chosen card has vanished. The records are separated and there on the pencil is the proper, marked, card.

Improved 20th Century Silk

By Manger

A flag is knotted to a red silk. The flag is then folded, leaving the red striped corner of the flag out. The folds are held together with a piece of silk thread. The prepared red silk, a blue silk, an envelope, a pencil and a duplicate flag are on your table.

The performer picks up the prepared red silk in his left hand, masking the secret bundle, and the blue silk in his right hand. He ties the blue to the red—really to the red corner of the concealed flag. The two silks are held at the point of knotting in the left hand. He asks a spectator to examine the envelope and to push a hole through the center of it with the pencil. He now puts the knotted silks in the en-

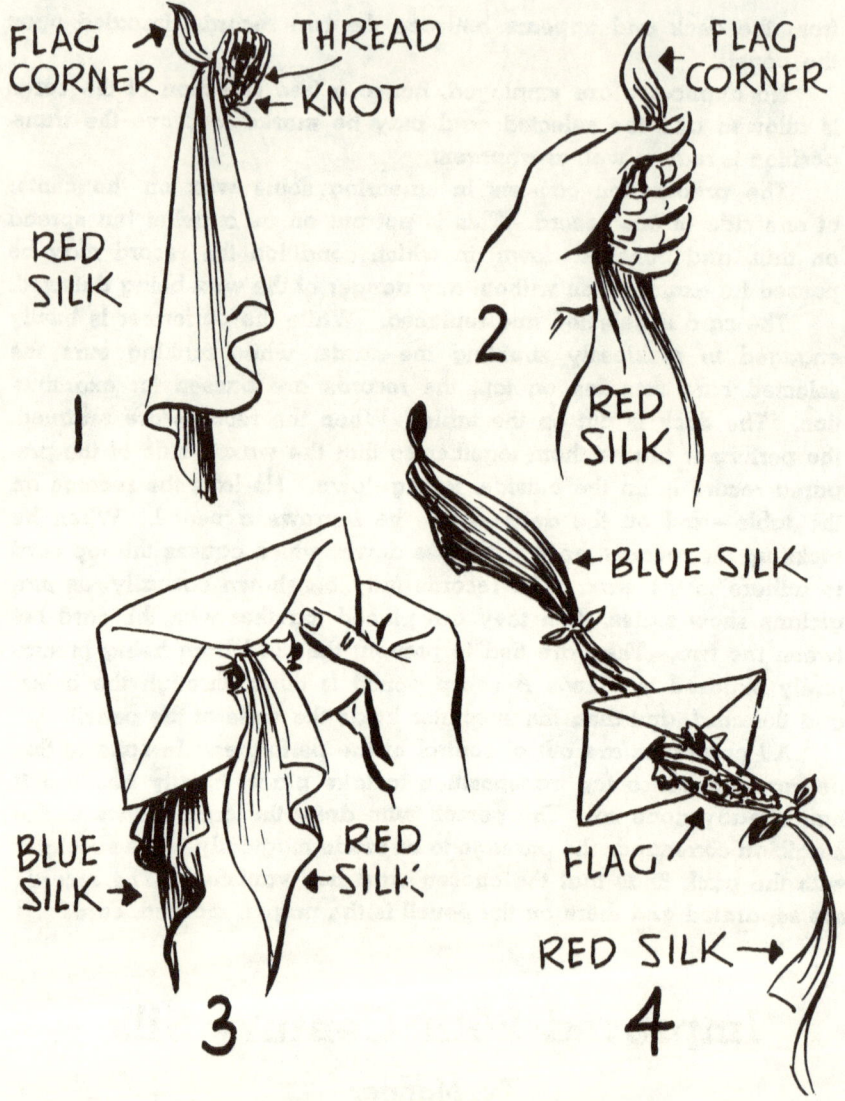

velopes, and shoves a corner of the blue silk out through one hole, a corner of the red out through the other.

The performer seals the envelope. The extending silks are pulled out further and a spectator holds them between his hands. The magician vanishes the duplicate flag by a body pull or some other piece of apparatus. The spectator is told to pull on the ends of the silks extending from the envelope. He does and the flag appears — knotted between the two silks. There is no clue to the mystery in the envelope. Everything may be examined.

The illustration makes the handling clear. Figure 1 shows how the flag and red silk are prepared, 2 illustrates how the red silk is held for the tying, 3 shows how the silks protrude from the envelope, 4 shows the climax as the flag appears.

The Five Card Trick

By Tom Osborne

Long Tack Sam showed me this trick years ago. He admitted that it wasn't his; so, after keeping the secret for these many years, I would like to pass it on.

The performer hands a deck to someone, and tells him to shuffle the cards and lay five cards, face down, on the table. The deck is returned to the performer. Now the magician invites a spectator to lift up one card, remember it, and replace it in its original position, all while the performer turns his head away.

The performer turns away for two reasons. First, it gives him an opportunity to wet the ball of his left thumb secretly with saliva,

Secondly, it conveys the impression that the performer isn't looking when the spectator sights the card. Actually the performer peeks so that he will know the position of the selected card.

Once the card is replaced, the performer swings around and gathers up the group. Suppose the middle card was lifted, then the magician picks up two of the other cards and puts them face down in his left hand as indicated in Figure 1. As he brings the third card, the chosen one, with his right hand from the table to his left hand, the left thumb moves across the present top card in his left hand, wetting the back. When the chosen card is put on the wet pack, only a firm pressure is necessary to make the two cards stick together. When all five cards are in the left hand, hold your hand as in Figure 2. With the right hand, reach up and withdraw the card nearest to the left thumb—the rear card, that is. Ask if that is the selected card. On being assured that it is not, drop it to the floor. Repeat with the next card. The next card will really be two cards stuck together, the selected card with its face out of view against the back of an indifferent card. Exercise a little care so that the two cards don't become separated. Drop the two as one on the floor as you did the others. Repeat the withdrawing and the question: "Is this your card?" with the last card.

Still holding your hand cupped as though it contained the fifth card, say: "Well, what was your card?" On being told, say: "That's what I thought." Brush both hands together. Apparently the selected card vanishes in thin air.

This vanish is an astonishing one for a lay audience. After you have acknowledged the audience's amazement, casually pick up the cards and go on with another trick.

Pip of a Pipe

By George Andrew

While the stunt of touching a piece of palmed flash paper on your cigarette is very good, it is far more effective with a pipe, when done as follows:

Pack your pipe lightly with a rather dry, crumbly tobacco. After it is burning well, palm a piece of crumpled black flash paper into the bowl. The paper should be big enough so that it doesn't fall down on the fire. The palming can be done in a very natural way as you grasp the bowl. Now you are ready to set it off at any time you wish by simply blowing into the pipe through the stem. Blow strongly enough to raise a few hot ashes and sparks up to the paper.

Not only will you find this very effective when the hands are nowhere near the pipe at the time of the flash, but the flash is not screened by the hand and is thus more startling.

It is very funny to use this at odd moments during an evening with some friends. Pretend to notice nothing out of the ordinary when the flashes occur.